THE TENTH TRAIL MARK

JOE LOOBY

ISBN: 979-8-9991301-8-1

Published by 10TH MOUNTAIN FILMS, LLC

Mount Pleasant, SC, USA

Printed in the United States of America

ALSO BY JOE LOOBY

THE TENTH SERIES

The Tenth Trail Mark — *the story of the men who climbed.* A WWII Novel of Courage, Sacrifice, and the 10th Mountain Division.

The Tenth Station — *the story of the man who taught them how to fight.* A WWI Novel of Love, Courage, and the Rock of the Marne.

The Tenth Command — *the story of the men who led them.* A WWII Novel of Leadership, Redemption, and the 10th Mountain Division.

PRAISE FOR THE TENTH TRAIL MARK

"A sweeping historical novel... the prose balances rugged realism with lyrical detail... the ending is intense and resonant."

— *FOREWORD* CLARION REVIEWS

What Readers Are Saying

"This deeply researched and beautifully written book shows how an Adirondack boy... becomes an expert and courageous mountain soldier... A must-read for historical fiction lovers."

— ELIZABETH, ★★★★★ AMAZON REVIEW

"More than just a war story; it's a deeply moving tribute to the human spirit... This isn't just a book you read; it's one you feel."

— ADK 46, ★★★★★ AMAZON REVIEW

CONTENTS

To my father, Jim Looby,
and the valiant men of the 10th Mountain Division.

And to Connie, my trail mark.

Definition:

Trail mark (noun) refers to any sign, symbol, or feature that indicates or guides a path or route along a trail, especially in outdoor, wilderness, or hiking environments.

Purpose:

To prevent getting lost

AUTHOR'S NOTE

This novel is a work of historical fiction inspired by the real events of the battles at Riva Ridge and Mount Belvedere in Italy during World War II. While I've taken creative liberties with aspects of the timeline, characters, and tactical details, the spirit of this story remains grounded in truth, respect, and admiration.

My father served with the 10th Mountain Division during this campaign. He fought in those mountains and was wounded in battle. His courage—and the courage of the men he served alongside—is something I carry with me. Writing this story is my way of honoring not just their bravery but the human experience behind the history: the fear, the grit, the humor, the heartbreak, and the extraordinary strength of ordinary men.

All the characters in this book are fictional. But none of their valor is. Every man portrayed here is treated as a hero—because they were.

To the veterans who fought in those mountains and to their families, thank you. This book is for you.

PROLOGUE: PART I

THE LINE (THE GREAT WAR)

July 14, 1918

Near Grevés Farm, France

The world was nothing but mud and thunder, a landscape torn into an inferno. The Germans had launched their final, desperate offensive, a massive assault aimed at shattering the Allied front.

Their artillery, relentless and merciless, tore apart the very sky, shredding communication lines and isolating First Lieutenant George P. Hays of the 10th Field Artillery.

With the German army attempting to break through, Hays's task was impossible: to hold the fracturing line together, a lifeline in a maelstrom of chaos.

He was the last thread, the sole courier between his battery, the command post, and two imperiled French units. There was no clear path, only an unforgiving terrain of craters and shrapnel.

He had to ride, not just as a messenger, but as a living trail mark through the storm.

He swung onto the saddle, the leather protesting. With a desperate kick, he spurred the horse into a gallop, driving straight into the geysers of exploding earth and shrieking steel. He charged through the murderous rain, a singular, unwavering force of will against unscalable odds.

Then, an abrupt quiet.

The storm's roar dulled, replaced by the rhythm of survival: his own pounding heart, the thud of hooves on ravaged earth. *Inhale.* The horse's straining lungs, a counterpoint to his own. *Exhale.*

A 90-pound shell screaming overhead became just wind. Shrapnel whining past his ear, a mere buzzing fly. There was only the ride—*inhale*—and the desperate, forward motion propelled by the bond between man and horse—*exhale*—a refusal to yield to the impossible.

He rode on, a driving force in the mud, past splintered carts, through brackish craters, past the shattered bodies of men he knew. He refused to see them.

He became a promise, a vital link. Each stride was a desperate lunge, a testament to sheer will, forging a path where none existed. Then, a shell landed too close.

A deafening roar shattered the fragile peace. The world erupted in earth and hot metal. The horse screamed, collapsing in a tangle of broken limbs and blood. Hays was thrown clear, the quiet replaced by a high, piercing ring.

A single, brutal thought cut through the ringing: The line must hold. Bloodied but unbowed, he scrambled to his feet, found another mount, and spurred it back into the heart of the storm.

Six more times, the fire found him—six more times, a horse died beneath him, its life swallowed by the blast. And six more times, severely wounded, Hays clawed his way from the wreckage, found a new mount, and plunged back into the chaos. He rode straight through the impossible—a defiance of survival itself.

For two days, First Lieutenant George P. Hays did not just ride the line; he was the line.

His unyielding spirit forged a path through the unscalable, a testament to a courage that would, decades later, guide another generation through mountains of ice and fire, to the very top of what was deemed impossible.

This was the first of many trails he would mark for those who dared to follow.

Twenty-seven years later, on the most agonizing day of his command, General George P. Hays would remember that impossible ride through a storm of steel.

He would remember it as he ordered his 10th Mountain soldiers to climb into their own inferno, to do what the world believed could not be done.

PROLOGUE: PART II

THE GOTHIC LINE (WORLD WAR II)

February 15, 1945

The Northern Apennines, Italy

By early 1945, the war in Italy had devolved into a brutal stalemate. Though the Allied advance had pushed northward for over a year, the cost had been immense. The 170,000-strong U.S. Fifth Army had been bled white during the agonizing battles to break the Gustav Line, culminating in the pyrrhic victory at Monte Cassino.

But that triumph brought no relief. The Germans had withdrawn to an equally daunting barrier—the Gothic Line—and it was here that the advance stalled, against a new line that refused to break.

The Gothic Line was a network of fortifications stretching across the rugged Apennine Mountains, a testament to the strategic genius of German Commander-in-Chief Albert Kesselring.

A masterful defensive strategist, Field Marshal Kesselring

had personally overseen its construction, creating a monster of rock and steel. He integrated hundreds of concrete-reinforced bunkers, intricate trench systems, and camouflaged artillery positions into the unforgiving terrain.

Natural caves were reinforced, and every position was designed to kill from multiple angles, creating a web of death where any advance was a suicide run.

The heart of this defense was a formidable four-part mountain complex.

It was anchored by **Riva Ridge**, a key 3.5-mile-long ridgeline with a chain of commanding peaks—Pizzo di Campiano, Cappel Buso, and others—that guarded the western approach to the central stronghold, **Mount Belvedere.** This fortress was reinforced by its twin peak, **Mount Gorgolesco**, and linked to **Mount della Torraccia**, which secured the eastern flank.

The German defenses were layered and lethal.

Forward outposts with scouts and machine guns served as an early warning system. The main lines were a web of bunkers and trenches, all zeroed in by hidden artillery and mortar units.

German spotters on the high peaks could direct fire with deadly precision, while minefields and barbed wire blanketed every logical approach. It was a Goliath, guarding the vital path to the Po Valley, the Alps, and Germany itself.

Against this Goliath of rock and steel, a "David" was being readied: Major General George P. Hays.

Hays assumed command of the 10th Mountain Division on November 23, 1944. He was not a distant figure from military history but a commander forged in the ongoing war, having landed on Normandy's beaches on D-Day plus one.

More than his rank, Hays carried the weight of a memory from the First World War. He was the man who had made that impossible horseback ride through a storm of steel, an act of "pure courage under unimaginable fire" that earned him the Medal of Honor.

That ride had seared a terrible knowledge into his soul: he understood the brutal arithmetic of artillery.

Now, twenty-seven years later, the weight of command demanded he send a new generation into their own inferno, and the memory of those seven dead horses was a constant, agonizing presence.

The Fifth Army was bleeding, its conventional tactics proving insufficient against Kesselring's fortress. The stalemate was claiming hundreds of lives weekly with no end in sight.

As Hays studied the topographical maps, the jagged lines of the Apennines rising like a dragon's spine, he knew this was different. This was vertical. This was a fortress of rock and ice.

But his men... they weren't conventional. He was about to ask them to do what no one else could.

To break this bloody impasse, a new, specialized approach was needed. It was into this grim landscape that the 10th Mountain Division, with its 14,000 highly trained soldiers, was quietly deployed.

Their unique capabilities in skiing, climbing, and cold-weather survival were the specialized tools the Fifth Army needed to tackle the impossible. The stage was now grimly set for their arrival. The plan was codenamed Operation Encore.

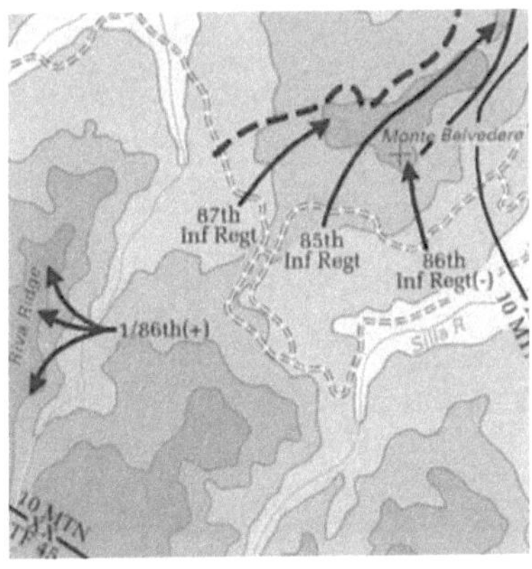

Map: Operation Encore

On the night of 15 February 1945, the first soldiers began their impossible climb to break the line.

This is their story.

INTRODUCTION

1931

Lake Placid, NY

Johnnie Grey was born on July 14, 1923, in the sweltering heat of summer, in a rugged corner of the Adirondacks where the air tasted of pine and the grit of the daily struggle of life. His worth wasn't measured in grades or sports but in the sharp crack of a squirrel shot clean from a branch or the silent, efficient way he made his way through the unforgiving mountain wilderness.

By the time he turned eight, the Great Depression, a cold, damp shroud, had rolled into their valley, clinging to the mountainsides and seeping into every home, chilling bones and crushing every budding hope. Survival wasn't a concept; it was daily bread. Even then, Johnnie could coax a meal from the leanest woods, hike alone through the forest, or find warmth where others shivered.

1

THE BOY

At 7 a.m. on a cold October morning in 1931, the roar of the yellow school bus shattered the quiet of the dirt road outside their cabin, a jarring intrusion into the morning's stillness. Johnnie, with his handmade slingshot tucked into his belt and a small pouch of stones in his pocket, waved the bus down with practiced ease.

Mr. Sandford, the World War I vet who drove the bus, his shoulders carrying an invisible weight, greeted him with a brief, weary nod.

The older man's prosthetic hand, a stark testament to a war wound, clanked against the metal doorframe as he pushed open the door, the sound dull and cold, an unambiguous reminder of a war Johnnie couldn't yet comprehend.

"Where you headed?" Mr. Sandford rasped, his voice gravelly, a puff of his breath clouding the frigid air.

"Intervales woods," Johnnie murmured, the word a small, white plume of frost.

"Might be squirrels up there. Or maybe I'll try the woods near the airfield today, see if any planes are flying."

Mr. Sandford nodded a flicker of understanding in his eyes. "Best of luck, son."

Johnnie and his six-year-old sister Allee boarded the bus. The air inside was heavy with the scent of damp wool and stale air. Some of the other boys huddled on the worn seats, weren't headed to school either. Their hands, although small, were rough and gripped an assortment of hunting tools, including BB guns, slingshots, and trapping gear.

The Lake Placid High School on Main Street was a luxury for families who still had enough to spare. Johnnie knew it was overcrowded; he'd seen the older kids practically spilling out the doors of the brick building on Main Street.

But his mom said Johnnie was "overflow," or something like that, which is why his classes were held in the basement of St. Eustace's Episcopal Church.

On the rare days he attended, that's where he ended up: in the church's cool, dim basement, a world apart from the sun-dappled forest. For Johnnie and others whose families barely made ends meet with what the land and their wits could provide, regular schooling was out of reach. Hunting served as a means of survival.

Johnnie didn't hunt with a BB gun, unlike some boys. BBs were a one-shot endeavor, and boxes of BBs cost money—money he didn't have, especially when he could get his main ammunition, smooth stones from the river, for free.

His tool was quieter, simpler, and more his own: a slingshot. He'd crafted it himself from a Y-shaped piece of ashwood he'd cut and sanded smooth, then polished with oil until it felt like a natural extension of his arm.

The elastic came from an old bicycle inner tube, carefully sliced into bands and tied to a small, weathered but sturdy leather pouch.

He took pride in it. Each night, he would check the bands for wear and wipe down the polished ashwood, the familiar weight—a comfort in his hand. It hit hard, and it was quiet—just a whisper through the air, followed by the sudden thump of impact. Perfect for the forests of the Adirondacks, where stealth mattered more than firepower.

Most days, he hunted squirrels—red ones mainly—using smooth granite stones gathered from the streambeds near his house. They were far more plentiful than rabbits and more straightforward to track through the trees.

Squirrels were erratic and fast, darting and doubling back in bursts of unpredictable energy, but Johnnie had learned their rhythms. He knew where to find them and how to wait.

Rabbits were different. Warier. Quieter. Harder to hit. They stuck to the brambles, hugging the edges of farm plots and clearings, ready to vanish at the slightest noise. Hunting one was a rare thing—and for that, Johnnie reserved his best shot. He had a single steel ball bearing polished to a gleam; he called it his "silver bullet."

He'd found it half-buried in the damp earth near the silent, rust-eaten gears of a colossal, abandoned machine at an old lumber mill deep in the woods—a place hushed now save for the wind sighing through rotting timbers and the faint, metallic tang of decay.

He and Allee sometimes ventured there, their hushed whispers swallowed by the vastness.

They'd dare each other to climb the giant, pulp-smelling wood chip piles, thrilling at the soft, tumbling slide to the bottom, their laughter a brief, bright sound in the stillness.

The silver bullet was his most prized possession, kept in a tattered cloth pouch deep in his pocket. He only pulled it out on clear, sunny days—days when he might have a real chance at spotting a cottontail.

He'd brought down sixty-three of them with it, but it never got routine.

Each shot counted. And after the rabbit was down, the real

challenge began: finding the silver bullet again. The sun helped. That was the trick.

He used the silver bullet only on bright days, knowing its polished surface would reflect just enough light to give itself away among the roots and leaves.

Sometimes, he'd spend more time searching for it than he had spent hunting. Still, it was worth it. He tapped his pocket often just to feel it there. Sometimes, he'd take it out and crush it in his palm—a habit, like biting your lip or cracking your knuckles.

In a time when a nickel could buy valuable things, and many families struggled to afford every meal, the ability to provide food in this way was not just a skill but a vital contribution to survival—a daily triumph against hardship that built profound self-reliance unknown to those in easier times.

As the bus rumbled past the turn-off for the old Intervales farm, its meadows now home to the growing ski jump, Johnnie signaled his stop. He and a few other boys, equally intent on the hunt, got off the bus.

Some days, he'd ride further, getting off near the Adirondack Airfield. The field, officially opened just the year before, was still mostly a vast expanse of grass in the woods.

But the chance to see an airplane, a true marvel in 1931, lumbering across the field and then miraculously lifting into the sky was a powerful draw—a glimpse of a world far removed from his daily hunt and worth it.

2

THE FOREST

Once off the bus, whether in the woods bordering the open fields of Intervales or the denser forest near the airfield, the wilderness swallowed Johnnie.

It was a familiar embrace of towering pines, sugar maples, stands of birch trees, and hushed snow. This was his realm, a silent world where every rustle, every snapped twig, held meaning.

He knew the game trails, the almost imperceptible pathways that others might overlook, the places where the squirrels and cottontails might hide. He moved quietly, his eyes sharp and ceaseless, scanning the tree canopy and the forest floor.

He watched the squirrels, their movements a blur of unpredictable energy: a dart, a freeze, a zig-zag sprint, then up a trunk. He studied their evasions, their instinctual survival dance, unknowingly etching their patterns and the subtle language of the wild into his very being.

By mid-morning, when the cold began to bite, he found a sheltered hollow. His canvas knapsack held a crust of bread, his trusty jackknife, some twine, a homemade fish hook, and his slingshot. That was enough.

With practiced ease, he pulled out his flint and steel, striking sparks onto a small pile of dry kindling and birchbark he'd collected. A tiny ember caught, then grew, coaxed by his breath into a flickering flame.

Soon, a small, defiant fire crackled, its warmth a precious solace against the gnawing chill. He ate his meager lunch alone, the profound silence broken only by the crackle of the fire and the distant caw of a crow.

Yet, even in these quiet moments, a faint shadow sometimes lingered. A sudden, unexplained chill would sweep over him, or the phantom scent of something acrid and burning would briefly taint the clean mountain air. These fleeting intrusions would vanish as quickly as they came, leaving him with only a vague unease he couldn't name.

As he chewed, his gaze drifted to his slingshot resting beside him, its ashwood frame smooth beneath his fingers. In his hand, it felt like an extension of his arm, a tool of survival. But in the quiet of the forest, it sometimes transformed. It wasn't just for squirrels or rabbits.

The Y-shaped wood became the stock of a rifle, and the leather pouch served as a magazine. He was a soldier, strong and brave, imagining himself sighting down the barrel at a distant, unseen enemy, just like the heroes in the war stories his father's friends sometimes whispered about.

He imagined himself in a far-off land, snow-covered mountains, and the roar of distant battles. He was there, with his father, a fleeting presence beside him. In his mind's eye, he was faster and more inventive, seeing the unseen dangers and deflecting the impossible.

He would pull his father to safety and shield him if needed. He would save him. The daydream was vivid, a poignant wish against the harsh reality of his world, a silent promise to a ghost he barely remembered.

He never asked his mother about the war or his dead father;

it was a quiet, heavy silence in their home he instinctively knew not to disturb.

Then, the cold would creep back in, the fire would dwindle, and the fantasy would recede, leaving him alone again, just Johnnie Grey, a boy with a slingshot, hunting for survival.

3

THE RIDE HOME

At 3:30 p.m., the familiar rumble of the yellow school bus echoed down the dirt road, a welcome sound signaling the end of another long day. Johnnie, emerging from the dense woods that bordered the road, waved it down.

Slung over his shoulder, a string tied through their legs, were four plump red squirrels—a decent haul, though less than he'd hoped. Their fur brushed against his worn jacket, providing a soft, almost imperceptible weight.

The other children, returning from Lake Placid High School, peered out the grimy windows, their faces pressed against the cold glass. Some stared with open curiosity at the boy who had made the day's kill. In contrast, others, particularly the older ones, offered quiet nods of understanding, acknowledging Johnnie's daily routine and the stark realities it represented.

The scent of woods, snow, and damp earth clung to him, a sharp difference from the faint chalk dust and ink that permeated the schoolhouse air. There was no doubt in the older boys' eyes: Johnnie was a legend in these parts, a master hunter.

The bus hissed to a stop, its air brakes sighing. Mr. Sandford, his eyes holding a distant weariness of old battles and a flicker of kindness that softened their depths, gave Johnnie a brief, knowing nod.

"Good day for it, son?" he asked, his voice a low rumble that seemed to vibrate with the bus's idling engine.

Johnnie offered a salute and a small, tired smile in reply, the day's effort weighing on him. Mr. Sandford, a childhood friend of Johnnie's father, understood the unspoken language of survival that dictated their lives. He recognized that Johnnie wasn't coming from school but from the woods—a daily journey for the family's sustenance that took precedence over formal schooling.

With a wink, a nod, and a half-salute, Mr. Sandford offered a subtle blessing. It was a silent conspiracy, born of necessity and compassion, acknowledging the boy's vital role.

"How's your mom doing, Johnnie?" he always asked, his voice softening slightly.

Sometimes, a small, discreet parcel—a bag of flour, a few extra potatoes, or a precious tin of tea—would find its way into Johnnie's hand as he disembarked, a quiet, unspoken act of support for his old friend's widow.

4

HOME - PART I

Their home, the small cabin off Cascade Road, was small but meticulously maintained, with every surface scrubbed and every blanket folded, serving as a testament to his mother's tireless efforts and unwavering dedication. She was a seamstress, her nimble fingers constantly at work, repairing and mending old clothes for neighbors who, like them, had little cash to buy new ones. The rhythmic hum of her treadle sewing machine was a constant soundtrack to their days, a quiet testament to her labor.

Their world operated on a system of intricate barter—a mended coat for a handful of dried beans, a patched dress for a few precious eggs, a newly hemmed pair of trousers for a small sack of cornmeal. Even the modest rent for the cabin was often settled this way, her skills a valuable currency in a time when actual money was a scarce, almost mythical commodity.

Still, everyone worked together, bound by a silent compact of mutual aid and shared hardship that united the community in a web of interdependence.

That evening, after a dinner of hearty stew, rich with the squirrel meat Johnnie had brought home and root vegetables from their small, resilient garden, the air was thick with the comforting scent of herbs and simmering bone broth. Johnnie's mother would bring out the worn primers and arithmetic books.

While Allee, having spent her day at school absorbing the day's lessons, often drifted off to sleep by the warmth of the fire, her tiny body curled under a quilt, Johnnie received his home-school lessons. His mother, her brow furrowed in concentration, her finger tracing the words on the page, would teach him reading and arithmetic, her voice soft but firm, ensuring he had the foundational knowledge that formal schooling denied him.

It was a tranquil ritual, with a flickering oil lamp casting long shadows that danced on the cabin walls as they navigated through words and numbers. The scent of woodsmoke and simmering stew filled the small cabin, creating a sanctuary against the encroaching darkness of the Depression.

One night, as they finished their meal, the last spoonfuls of stew scraped from their bowls, Allee piped up, her eyes wide with the wonder of a recently learned fact, her youthful voice bright.

"Miss Fairchild told us today about Lewis and Clark, and the Corps of Discovery—" she exclaimed, her enthusiasm infectious. "When they went out West, they saw herds and hordes of squirrels in the tree canopy, heading south. Like birds migrating for the winter. They were overrun by squirrels. She said it was an amazing sight, like the trees were alive with them."

Mrs. Grey looked away from the squirrel meat in Johnnie's bowl, her attention turning to the window. Outside, the wind sighed through the forest that seemed to dissolve into the encroaching gloom, the air chilling with the coming night.

Staring into the deepening twilight, a familiar ache tightened in her chest. She murmured, "I remember when squirrels were so plentiful that when times turned lean, folks just turned to 'Tree Chicken.' But now...' Her voice faltered, trailing into a mere whisper to herself against the shadows, the words heavy as the falling night, 'I fear there'll be none left. For anyone."

Johnnie, who had been quietly picking at a bone, nodded slowly. He knew what she meant. He sensed it deeply in the growing challenges of his hunts, in the extended hours he spent tracking, and in the increasingly frantic searches for even a single target.

"It seems to be getting harder and harder to find them," he observed, his voice low, a quiet confirmation of his mother's fears. "Last year, I'd average six a day, easy. This year, I'm lucky if I get three, and I know I'm a much better hunter and shot now than I was then."

The dwindling numbers were a silent alarm bell ringing in the quiet woods, a harbinger of even leaner times to come, a chilling premonition of the scarcity that gripped their world.

For six days a week, except Sundays when the family would catch a ride into town for church, this was Johnnie's life. He was eight years old—hunting every day and studying every night—until one day, the Olympics came to town.

5

THE SNOWBALL FIGHT - PART I

One cold February morning in 1932, Johnnie and Allee waved the bus down with a practiced ease. Mr. Sandford greeted them the way he always did, their routine, a monotony born of necessity in the harsh world in which they now lived.

"Where you headed today, Johnnie?" Mr. Sandford asked.

"School, Mr. Sandford," Johnnie announced, a surprising answer. "Heard the Olympics are in town."

Mr. Sandford's eyebrows rose slightly, a flicker of something akin to amusement, perhaps even a touch of shared longing, in his tired eyes. "Well, I'll be. Get on then."

He waved Johnnie aboard, the bus groaning under the weight of its young, quiet passengers, each wrapped in layers of worn wool against the biting cold. As the bus rumbled towards Main Street, the usual somber quiet of the town was replaced by an unexpected, almost bewildering, cacophony. Main Street itself was transformed.

Huge, pristine snowbanks, piled high by recent plows and shovels, rose along the sidewalks. Fancy cars, long and gleaming with polished chrome and dark, expensive paint—

Packards, even Cadillacs—lined the curbs, their presence a vivid counterpoint to the usual utilitarian Ford Model As or older, work-worn trucks of the locals.

These were the out-of-towners' cars, brought in for the Olympics, and they looked completely out of place against the backdrop of the Depression-era storefronts.

And then, the sight that truly stunned them: adults, typically burdened by the grim realities of the Great Depression, their faces etched with worry and the constant struggle for survival, were engaged in a full-blown snowball fight. Their laughter, surprisingly uninhibited and joyous, echoed off the snow-laden buildings, a sound so out of place it felt almost magical.

But these weren't just any adults. These were strange adults, their faces flushed with an uncharacteristic abandon. Some had sharp, unfamiliar angles; others held broad, open smiles rarely seen on the town's weary residents.

They spoke a vibrant tapestry of guttural German, lilting French, clipped English, melodic Italian, sharp Japanese, and resonant Norwegian, each tongue a foreign melody that added to the bewildering spectacle.

They darted out from behind the fancy cars, lobbing snowballs with surprising ferocity, then retreating behind the vehicles when hit, only to dart out again, their foreign words mingling with shouts of mock outrage.

Johnnie, captivated by the spectacle, lowered his window, the cold air rushing in, allowing him to see the strange faces better and hear the unfamiliar languages. Just then, a rogue snowball, thrown with surprising force, sailed through the open window and splattered directly against Mr. Sandford's cheek, eliciting a surprised yelp.

Mr. Sandford, initially shell-shocked, seemed to stiffen. But then, a faint, almost forgotten spark of his old fighting spirit, perhaps from the trenches of a distant war, returned to his eyes.

He pressed on, driving the bus straight through the swirling white chaos.

When they reached the end of the street, he pulled the bus over with a decisive jerk, threw open the door and, with a grin that seemed to crack the lines of his weary face, declared, "Alright boys! Get 'em!"

It wasn't a command so much as an invitation to reclaim a piece of lost childhood, a momentary reprieve from the harshness of their lives.

Most of the kids, startled by the sudden, unprecedented command, froze. They got off the bus and huddled between parked cars, their small figures almost swallowed by the shadows, too timid to move against the adults, their instincts screaming caution.

But Johnnie, with the natural, unthinking instinct of a squirrel darting through the woods, didn't hesitate. He had spent his life navigating unpredictable terrain, and this felt no different. He launched himself into the fray, weaving down the street, changing pace and direction frequently, his movements a peculiar, unconventional, yet incredibly effective run.

He dipped, dodged, and spun, throwing snowballs with practiced precision from the makeshift pouch he'd made by lifting the bottom of his shirt.

His eyes, sharp and observant, constantly scanning for targets and openings, caught sight of another boy across the street—a shock of dirty blond hair escaping his cap—doing the exact same thing, mirroring his erratic, effective movements with uncanny similarity.

Their eyes met across the swirling white, a silent, electric connection forming amid the chaos. In that shared glance, a spark ignited a quiet understanding that transcended the noise and flying snow, a feeling of finding a missing piece, a kindred spirit.

Without a word, they exchanged a nod, an unspoken pact

that felt as old and true as the mountains themselves, forged in the heat of a spontaneous, joyful battle.

Johnnie and the new boy became a blur, darting and weaving, their throws precise and relentless. They moved as one, a small but unstoppable force, pelting the unsuspecting adults, grabbing snow off cars, and making new balls on the run when their stash got low or ran out.

Some men, dressed in their finest, often ill-fitting, fur coats, looked particularly bewildered as cold, wet snowballs found their mark, splattering against their expensive attire. The air was filled with shouts of surprise, yelps of mock outrage, and the continued, surprising laughter of the participants.

Suddenly, Mrs. Zypynski, the baker known for her stern demeanor but tasty pastries, emerged from her shop, ready to angrily yell at the unruly children. At first, she was shocked to see that many players were adults, not the schoolchildren she was used to berating.

But before a single word could escape her lips, a stray snowball, thrown by the new boy with a mischievous grin, exploded against her chest. With a huff of indignation and a splatter of snow, she marched back inside, doubtless to call the police, her fury a comical counterpoint to the general revelry.

In the swirling snow and the joyous chaos, a profound shift occurred in Johnnie's mind. He wasn't just playing a game; he was fighting. And he wasn't alone. The new boy, his silent ally, moved with the same fierce determination and unpredictable agility.

The fancy cars, the strange languages, the foreign faces—they weren't just Olympic visitors anymore. They were the opposition.

And Johnnie, with the new boy by his side, was a soldier.

He no longer saw himself as a solitary boy with a slingshot imagining battles but as an actual combatant defending his town and home from these others.

The Great War, a distant, unspoken terror in his father's generation, was now a vivid, present reality, played out in the snow-covered streets of Lake Placid, with him and his new friend on the front lines.

'This is it,' he thought, a cold thrill running through him. 'This is what it feels like.' This wasn't just a snowball fight; it was their war, and they were fighting it together.

The foreign adults, many of whom had been hit squarely by Johnnie and the new boy's relentless barrage, seemed to decide enough was enough. A murmur went through their ranks, and then, with surprising speed, they began to converge, racing towards the end of the street.

They formed a ragged but determined line, stretching across the width of Main Street, effectively blocking Johnnie and the new boy's path.

There were at least a dozen of them, perhaps more, their faces now less amused and more intent, their foreign words taking on a sharper, more challenging tone.

Johnnie and the new boy skidded to a halt, severely outnumbered, their snowball pouches emptying, their eyes darting between the formidable line of adults and the rapidly shrinking escape routes. A silent question passed between them: do they rush the line or find another way?

The tension cracked when, moments later, the cops arrived. In a heavy, blue wool coat, a cop turned the corner, blowing his whistle with a shrill, piercing sound that cut through the joyful chaos like a knife.

The snowball fight instantly dissolved.

The laughter died, shouts ceased, and people dropped their snowballs like hot coals, dispersing like startled pigeons, melting into the shops and alleys, leaving only scattered snow and a lingering sense of exhilaration.

The new boy, quick as a fox and seemingly familiar with the local authorities, grabbed Johnnie's arm and pulled him off

Main Street; they ran up the Hayes Street hill past St. Eustace's Episcopal Church to Hillcrest Avenue, the nicest street in town.

The new boy said, "I'm Edgar Darby; what's your name?" Johnnie replied, "Johnnie Grey." Edgar said, "Nice to meet you, Johnnie. Everyone calls me Darby."

Darby's house was the prettiest and most prominent on the street, with a sign in front that said "Dr. Edgar P. Darby, M.D." Darby didn't look like one of the kids from the church basement classes.

Johnnie reckoned Darby must be one of the St. Agnes boys he heard about from the Catholic school over on Saranac Avenue.

6

THE DARBYS' HOUSE

Inside the house, Darby's mother, a kind-faced woman with a warm smile that seemed to chase away the last vestiges of the cold, greeted them with a knowing look, a silent acknowledgment of their recent escapade.

Soon, the boys were huddled by a crackling fire, the scent of burning wood filling the air. They sipped steaming mugs of hot cocoa, the sweetness a welcome contrast to the cold outside, and devoured thick turkey sandwiches.

Their woolen gloves, hats, and boots, damp from the snow, warmed slowly by the fire, releasing a comforting, earthy aroma. In that moment, surrounded by warmth and the quiet hum of a welcoming home, Johnnie felt a profound sense of belonging he rarely experienced.

From that day on, Johnnie and Darby were nearly inseparable, their friendship as strong and enduring as the Adirondack peaks, a bond forged in shared mischief and the unexpected joy of a winter's day.

Their adventures continued, a blur of shared secrets, daring explorations, and the quiet understanding only true friends possess.

Johnnie soon met Dr. Darby, the father of Darby, a man of quiet wisdom and keen observation. Dr. Darby, hearing of the boys' escapades and, more importantly, understanding the history and struggles of Johnnie's family during those lean years, decided to intervene. Moved by their spirit and recognizing their innate resourcefulness, he leveraged his connections to get them jobs as gophers at the Olympics.

It was humble work, running errands, fetching supplies, and assisting wherever needed around the Olympic Center, as well as inside the high school, which had been partly converted into dressing rooms and preparation areas for the athletes.

Johnnie, hauling a crate of blankets through a hallway that echoed with unfamiliar shouts and smelled strongly of chalk, floor polish, and bathroom cleaner, joked to Darby, "Hey, I made it to school." Darby laughed.

For Johnnie, the work was a lifeline.

He made twenty-five cents a day, a small sum by most standards, but to him, it was a fortune.

He had never felt prouder than when he brought that first gleaming quarter home to his mom and baby sister, Allee; the coin felt heavy and significant in his palm, a tangible sign of his contribution, a small victory against the gnawing hunger of the Depression.

Years later, on the most brutal day of his life, he would remember that magical day when he met Edgar Darby.

7

THE OLYMPICS

1932

Before the war, before the ropes and rifles and the grim realities of combat, there was snow. Endless, pristine snow blanketed the Adirondacks in a hushed, magical silence.

It was 1932, and Lake Placid, their quiet, isolated hometown, buzzed with an electrifying anticipation that vibrated through every street and home.

The Winter Olympics had arrived, a dazzling spectacle descending upon their frozen landscape. And with them, a rare glimpse into a broader, more glamorous world.

For two local boys—Johnnie Grey and Edgar Darby—it was an opportunity to be part of something monumental, to see athletes from distant lands and witness feats of strength and grace they'd only read about in newspapers.

They weren't athletes. They were workers—small, nimble, and eager, their young bodies already toughened by endless hikes, by hauling firewood through deep snow, by the constant demands of a life lived close to the unforgiving peaks.

Runners, shovelers, errand boys—they took on anything the Olympic Committee required, their energy boundless.

By day, their small figures could be seen shoveling fresh snow from ice rinks or ferrying messages between foreign officials bundled in fur coats, their languages exotic and intriguing, their accents a symphony of unknown places.

By night, exhausted but exhilarated, they'd lean against fences, their faces flushed from the cold, catching fleeting glimpses of races and medals, their faces lit by the warm glow of torchlight and the satisfying crunch of boots on packed snow.

"Think we'll ever be out on that ski hill?" Johnnie mused once, his voice barely a whisper against the crowd's murmur, watching a Swiss skier carve a perfect, impossibly fluid descent down a mountain face, a streak of color against the white. His heart ached with a longing he couldn't name.

Darby smirked, his breath a white cloud in the air. "We'll be climbing to the top of that run before they even finish packing up the podiums." His confidence was solid, a counterpoint to Johnnie's quiet wonder.

They became unofficial ambassadors of the village, picking up broken phrases of French and German from the athletes, their young ears surprisingly adept at mimicking the foreign sounds.

This is when Johnnie met a man named Rolf Monsen, a Norwegian American, his eyes twinkling with an old wisdom that seemed to hold the secrets of the mountains. Rolf, dressed in the finest wool ski sweater Johnnie had ever seen, noticed the boy, a small figure with an intense gaze, staring at his skis with a quiet longing in his eyes.

"You ever tried?" Rolf asked, his accent thick and warm, handing Johnnie an old pair of skis and poles. "They're old," he said, the wood cracked at the tail and scratched on top from countless descents, "but if you fix them, they'll help you learn how to fly."

Johnnie's fingers, accustomed to the feel of birch bark and squirrel fur, traced the splintered edge of the ski, a thrill running through him. He looked at Darby, a silent question passing between them.

Together, they took the skis to Darby's basement, a place of comforting warmth and the scent of old wood. There, they set about sawing them down to a boy's size, carefully cutting away the broken parts in the process. They tightened the metal edges and filed them sharp with a rhythmic scrape that filled the quiet space. They used an iron to melt and apply hot wax, the sweet, earthy smell filling the air.

Then they took them to the hill. For weeks, they shared the single pair of skis, taking turns, with each descent a lesson and each fall a shared laugh.

8

NEW SKIS

Then, for his birthday, Darby got a pair of skis. Johnnie was amazed. Darby's skis were brand new, unused, not a scratch on their shiny surface, gleaming under the basement light. He ran a finger over the smooth, unblemished wood, a clear difference from the patched-up pair they'd shared.

Johnnie's grin stretched wide; now they could race side by side down the slopes.

Darby would always stop, during their runs, breathless, his face alight, to ask, "How'd I look?" "That jump?" "How fast was I going?" Johnnie, equally winded, would just grin and nod, already eager for the next run.

The new skis, however, did make Johnnie think about the differences between kids like him—in the church basement if they even saw the inside of a school—and the kids in town.

Darby, for instance, attended St. Agnes Catholic School, which Johnnie figured was a grand place with authentic desks and blackboards for everyone, and played basketball on some weekends.

But these were the only differences that made Johnnie a bit jealous—the ones that kept them apart.

9

SEE YOU AT THE TOP

It became their most cherished routine. After the solemn quiet of Sunday church, which settled deep in Johnnie's bones, Johnnie and Darby would make their way to the semi-abandoned ski jump hill. They knew Rolf was often there, practicing even on his "off" days, his dedication to skiing seemingly endless.

The hill, a relic of the recent Olympics, was a magnet for the town's children, a place where the air vibrated with shouts and laughter. Kids would toboggan and sled down its slopes, sending up plumes of snow, while a few, like Johnnie and Darby, would strap on skis.

Their races down the hill were legendary among the local kids. Sometimes, they'd carve graceful turns, mimicking the Olympians they'd watched with awe. Other times, they'd try daring tricks, sending sprays of snow into the air, much to the delight of their makeshift audience.

The goal was always the same: the first one to the bottom yelled, "See you at the top!" a challenge, a promise, and an invitation for the breathless scramble back up the slope.

They'd race back up, their young lungs burning, their legs

pumping, fueled by pure, unadulterated joy. Lost in the simple pleasure of the moment, every race, every tumble, every push up the hill steadily built their leg strength and honed their skiing and hiking technique.

"You know," Darby panted one afternoon, as they reached the top, leaning on their skis, "my dad says Rolf Monsen is America's greatest skier. He competed in the Olympics, you know. He was ranked sixth best in the world back in 1928. My dad says with all the training he's been doing this season, he has a shot at medaling in 1936."

Johnnie's eyes widened, and he looked at the unassuming man who patiently gave him a pointer or two every Sunday with new, profound awe. He had known Rolf was good, but this was a revelation.

Just then, Rolf Monsen appeared at the crest of the hill, a faint smile on his face. The boys immediately hushed, a respectful silence falling over them.

"Mr. Monsen," Johnnie began, his voice a little shy, "what's the secret to becoming a great skier?"

Rolf chuckled, his eyes sparkling. Just as he was about to respond, a group of officials shouted to him from the lodge below. "Monsen! We need you!" rang out from the lodge below.

He turned, waving a hand in acknowledgment. "Falling!" Rolf shouted back to the boys, his voice carrying on the crisp air as he skied away. "The secret is falling!"

Johnnie and Darby looked at each other, puzzled. Falling? That didn't make any sense.

But as they watched Rolf glide effortlessly down the slope, they knew there was more to it than met the eye.

10

RISING

1936-1938

As Johnnie honed his skills on the slopes, he slowly began to realize that Rolf Monsen was more than an Olympic athlete; he was a national figure. That realization solidified in 1936 when, despite a debilitating injury keeping him from competing in the German Winter Olympics, Rolf's national stature was undeniable.

Johnnie, devouring sparse reports in discarded newspapers, saw photos of Rolf proudly serving as the United States flag bearer during the opening ceremony. From those same delayed accounts, he pieced together the story of Adolf Hitler's chilling propaganda display at the Games.

Rolf's presence on that world stage, representing his country amidst such pageantry, transformed him in Johnnie's mind into a man whose purpose transcended mere athletic skill. It hinted at a larger world beyond the Adirondacks—a world of grander conflicts and duties that echoed the vague soldierly daydreams of his youth.

After the Olympics, Rolf returned to Lake Placid, and the mountain safety lessons he imparted began gaining national recognition. In 1938, that movement took on a formal name when Charles Minot 'Minnie' Dole founded the National Ski Patrol.

Dole's inspiration was deeply personal: a serious ski injury and a friend's tragic death had brutally underscored the dire need for organized mountain rescue.

For Johnnie, these developments were an affirmation, a sign that his path was converging with a larger purpose. The skills he was perfecting—navigating treacherous terrain, understanding snow conditions, assisting others—were no longer just for survival or sport; they were now formally recognized as vital for safety and rescue.

This quiet calling felt like a natural extension of his innate understanding of the wilderness, subtly setting the stage for a future where his unique mountain skills would be needed for a purpose far more significant and perilous.

Quietly, in the heart of the Adirondacks, the seeds of a mountain soldier were taking root.

ONE AFTERNOON in late September 1938, while running errands for his mother in town, Johnnie saw a stack of the *Lake Placid News* fresh off the press. The headline, in big, bold letters, screamed:

Munich Pact Signed: Europe Breathes Uneasy Sigh of Relief

He didn't understand all the names—Chamberlain, Daladier—but he understood the feeling he saw on the faces of the men in town: a deep-seated hope that the horrors of the Great War wouldn't be repeated.

The conflicting reports were confusing. Just a week later,

another headline quoted a man named Churchill who called the pact a "total and unmitigated defeat."

That evening, as Mr. Sandford was dropping off a parcel, Johnnie heard him speaking with his mother by the road.

"Peace for our time," Mr. Sandford said, his voice heavy with skepticism. "I've heard that song before. You don't make peace with a bully by giving him what he wants. That Churchill fellow, he sees it for what it is."

Johnnie listened as the bus rumbled away, the words leaving a chill that had nothing to do with the autumn air.

The world was bigger and more complicated than he had imagined, and the uneasy peace felt less like a resolution and more like the quiet before a storm.

11

SKI PATROL

1939-1941

By the time he was sixteen, Johnnie could glide through the forest twice as fast as most men could run on flat ground, his movements as fluid and silent as the falling snow.

Rolf Monsen had taught him the fine points—the subtle art of edge control that allowed him to carve perfect arcs and the precise steps of first aid that would help a fallen skier. But the rest, the deep, intuitive connection, came from the mountains.

So, when the Lake Placid Ski Patrol began looking for winter volunteers, Rolf didn't hesitate.

"He's young," Rolf told the patrol captain, his voice carrying the weight of his convictions, a quiet authority that brooked no argument, "but he's mountain-born. He knows these peaks better than any map."

Johnnie joined the Lake Placid Ski Patrol.

While Johnnie's local patrol was a close-knit group, it was part of a larger, dedicated network. Across the country, the National Ski Patrol, even in those early war years, comprised a few hundred to perhaps a thousand active patrollers like Johnnie, spread across various local units—a small but highly skilled cadre of skiers who knew the mountains.

They gave Johnnie a bright red parka, its color a vivid departure from the white landscape, along with a heavy pack filled with blankets, ponchos, bandages, splints, and a pair of surplus snowshoes for emergencies.

His new gear served as a badge of honor that he wore with quiet pride. It was the first new piece of clothing Johnnie could remember getting.

He was the youngest patroller on the mountain, and his presence initially drew grumbles from some of the seasoned skiers—old-timers who'd seen it all—about "the new boy."

But these doubts quickly faded.

When the weather turned foul, sudden blizzards engulfed the peaks and the trails, and visibility dropped to a frosty white while the wind howled like a banshee. It was Johnnie they followed, his unerring instinct serving as their compass and his quiet confidence acting as a steady beacon.

He knew the terrain in a way maps didn't show—where the powder drifted too deep, hiding treacherous drops that could snap a leg; where the relentless wind carved ice into hidden traps, slick and unforgiving; and where a broken binding meant a long, difficult drag downhill, a silent test of endurance that pushed men to their limits.

More than once, Johnnie pulled a fallen skier back from a hidden ledge, his grip firm, his movements efficient, his face grim with concentration. One memorable time, he transported a man with a sprained ankle a half-mile on a makeshift sled he'd lashed together with pine boughs over the man's skis, his muscles screaming, but his will unyielding; the man's grateful whispers a small reward.

At night, in the warming hut, the scent of the fire mingling with damp wool, he'd listen more than he spoke as others recounted the day's rescues like cherished legends, their voices rough with exhaustion and pride.

What mattered most to Johnnie wasn't the stories but the quiet assurance that he could help. That when things went wrong, and the mountain's vast indifference threatened to claim someone, someone would come looking, and that someone might just be him.

High on the slopes, with the wind cutting sharp and frost coating his goggles, blurring his vision, Rolf's words echoed in his mind, a mantra whispered in the frigid air: "The mountain's trail owes you nothing, but if you learn to see it, feel it, listen to it—it will teach old and important lessons."

Johnnie never forgot that.

Wearing the ski patrol patch and parka with pride, the vibrant color a beacon against the snow, he skied with purpose, his skills now recognized and directed toward service, with each experience a profound lesson, a waypoint guiding him toward an unknown but meaningful future.

Each trail he took was a lesson in itself. Because someday, he knew, he'd need every skill the mountain had taught him.

12

FALLING

One Saturday, Rolf, Johnnie, and Darby were up on Mount Van Hoevenberg, enjoying the crisp air and the quiet rhythm of the slopes. Rolf was demonstrating a new technique—a subtle shift of weight that allowed for a smoother, faster turn—when a jeep churned up snow as it pulled up to the warming hut below.

Two men in crisp Army uniforms, their faces stern and unsmiling, stepped out and headed directly towards the hut.

Johnnie and Darby exchanged worried glances. They were young, and to them, men in Army uniforms usually meant trouble or, at the very least, a serious conversation. Had Rolf done something wrong? Was he in some kind of trouble?

The thought that these men had come to take Rolf away, to disrupt their peaceful Saturdays of learning, filled them with a quiet dread.

They watched, hushed, as Rolf, seemingly unfazed, greeted the men and disappeared with them into the hut.

The afternoon passed slowly, filled with an unspoken tension. Johnnie and Darby kept glancing at the hut, expecting Rolf to emerge at any moment, perhaps in handcuffs.

But he didn't. As twilight bled into a premature, icy night, and the ski patrol began helping to close up the hut and rope off the trails, Rolf finally reappeared, his face thoughtful but not grim.

"Mr. Monsen, what happened?" Johnnie blurted out, unable to hold back his curiosity any longer. Darby nodded eagerly beside him.

Rolf smiled, a faint, distant look in his eyes. "Those men were from the Army," he began, his voice low, "and they were very interested in how we do things in Norway. You see, back in my home country, our Army is trained to fight in the mountains, in the cold winter weather. Men with rifles on skis, who can climb straight up cliffs, move silently through the snow."

Johnnie and Darby stared, their mouths slightly agape. Skiers with rifles? Climbing cliffs? It was a concept so foreign, so incredible, it seemed like something out of a storybook. They had never heard of such a thing.

The American Army hadn't either, until recently, Rolf continued a hint of pride in his voice. "There's a man, Charles Minot 'Minnie' Dole, the head of our National Ski Patrol. For several years, he had been writing to President Roosevelt and the Army, urging them that the United States needed to establish a Winter Army similar to Norway's. They came here today to ask me if I would assist them in doing that."

Rolf paused, looking at the boys with a mix of excitement and sadness in his eyes. "So, the Army is coming to Lake Placid. And in a few weeks, I will have to go away for a while to help them set up Pine Camp, near Fort Drum, to support their mountain training in the Adirondacks."

Johnnie and Darby were excited at the idea of a winter army, but a pang of sadness quickly followed. They recognized that their time with Rolf, their patient and wise mentor, was drawing to a close. He was being called away to bigger things, to a purpose far grander than teaching two boys to ski.

Realizing this might be their last chance for a while, Johnnie remembered the puzzling answer Rolf had given them a while ago.

"Mr. Monsen," he asked, his voice earnest, "what did you mean when you said the secret to becoming a great skier is 'falling'?"

Rolf's eyes softened.

He knelt, drawing a simple diagram in the snow with his ski pole. "It's like a parable, boys. In skiing, if you're not falling, you're not learning. It means you're not pushing yourself to see what the limits are. You're staying safe, staying in your comfort zone. But to become truly great, you have to find those limits. You have to push past them, even if it means tumbling in the snow. And then, you need to find ways to go past them—ways that no one before ever thought of."

He looked at them, a profound message in his gaze. "That's how you become great, not just in skiing, but in anything."

13

THE LOST TROOP

One slow Saturday afternoon, without warning, a terrible swirling maelstrom of snow—a true squall that rapidly escalated into a blinding blizzard—roared over Mount Van Hoevenberg.

Most outsiders, unfamiliar with the Adirondacks' brutal temperament, never truly grasped the severity of its storms: hurricanes in the summer and fall and winter blizzards that rivaled summer hurricanes but with snow, earning a local peak the ominous name "Hurricane Mountain."

But the locals knew. They took the weather with a solemn reverence, their history filled with whispered tales of the unfortunate or untrained who had perished in nature's unforgiving embrace. The familiar landscape vanished, swallowed by a furious whiteout that rendered visibility to mere feet.

It was into this sudden, unforgiving tempest that a Boy Scout troop from Delmar, NY, had unwittingly hiked along the cross-country trails. Their leader, taken ill, had stayed behind, leaving them vulnerable.

As twilight bled into a premature, icy night, they were presumed lost, their day-hike supplies woefully inadequate for the ordeal. From the warming hut, Rolf, his face grim with concern, quickly sent the ski patrolmen, including Johnnie, into the teeth of the storm.

Johnnie moved through the swirling snow like a phantom, his movements fluid and silent, a ghost in the white chaos. Where marked trails disappeared under drifts and the air stung with ice, his innate understanding of the forest became his compass; he knew the trees, their silent language guiding him through the deepening gloom. After what felt like an eternity, he stumbled upon them—a huddled, shivering mass of boys, their faces pale with fear and cold, their hope flickering like dying embers.

After introductions and a sobering inventory of the scouts' meager survival gear, Johnnie's voice, though hoarse from the biting wind, cut through their chattering, carrying an undeniable authority. "Alright, listen up!"

His gaze swept over the desperate young faces, settling on two older boys. "Darcy! Tyler! You two are in charge of teams. Darcy, you and half the boys start gathering every bit of dry firewood you can find. Move fast, we need a fire, now! Tyler, you take the other half. We're constructing a lean-to to shield us from this wind. Find sturdy branches, pine boughs, anything for shelter."

Driven by Johnnie's calm urgency, the boys sprang into action, their fear momentarily eclipsed by a sense of purpose. They worked with desperate energy, their numb fingers fumbling but persistent, until a small, defiant fire finally flickered to life, its warmth a precious solace against the crushing cold.

Johnnie then lashed the ponchos from his pack over their makeshift lean-to, creating a better barrier against the wind and snow, and handed his spare blankets to the youngest, most shivering boys.

He then taught them to stuff snow into their aluminum

canteens, which they carefully placed near the fire to melt the snow.

"Because," he explained, his voice low but clear, "everyone knows you don't try and eat snow directly for hydration - it will chill you further and takes more energy than you get back."

The scouts from the city, though nodding in understanding, exchanged wide-eyed glances; this was news to them. They had been eating snow all afternoon after their canteens ran dry.

Around the hastily fashioned lean-to, they huddled together, sharing what little warmth the fire offered, the long, terrifying night slowly giving way to a pre-dawn light.

As the first faint streaks of dawn appeared, a new sound cut through the wind—the rhythmic crunch of skis and snowshoes on deep snow. Rolf, leading a team of local men and the troop's frantic scoutmaster, appeared like apparitions, pulling a sled laden with snowshoes. Rolf had followed the signal and found them.

Johnnie, with a flash of his mentor's wisdom, had instructed the boys to continuously feed the fire, not just with wood but with birch bark for bright, tall flames and wet leaves to create thick, smoky plumes. He knew Rolf would see the smoke.

With the new snowshoes distributed, the tired but alive troop marched through the deep snow, leaving the mountain's icy grip behind.

THE RESCUE of the lost troop solidified Johnnie's reputation on the mountain, but the quiet heroism of the ski patrol felt increasingly small against the news rumbling from across the ocean.

Rolf would bring discarded copies of *The New York Times* to the warming hut, the headlines stark and grim. First, in the autumn of '39, it was **Britain and France Declare War**. A year later, in September 1940, the news was even more dire: **London Bombed as Germany Launches Relentless Air Assault.**

The grainy photographs of smoke-choked London skies and rubble-strewn streets felt a world away, yet the fear was palpable.

"They're fighting for their lives over there," Rolf said quietly one afternoon, his gaze fixed on a photo of a London firefighter. "It's not a matter of *if* we'll be in it, boys. It's a matter of *when.*" The words hung in the air, heavy as the coming snow.

14

THE WINTER WAR

One crisp autumn evening in 1940, with the scent of wood smoke lingering in the air—a comforting aroma that usually signaled peace—Johnnie found Darby by the lake, skipping stones as they had done a thousand times before.

The usual easy silence between them, a silence born of deep understanding, was broken by Johnnie's restless energy, a nascent yearning for something more, something beyond the familiar confines of their valley.

Darby skipped a flat stone, watching it skim across the water five times before sinking. "Hey, you want to hear something?" Darby began, his voice suddenly serious, a shift from their usual light banter.

He pulled a worn, folded copy of *Life Magazine* from his jacket pocket, its pages dog-eared and creased. "I've been reading about this. The Winter War."

Johnnie frowned. "The Winter War. What's that?"

Darby opened the magazine to a spread with maps and bold headlines, practically vibrating with excitement.

"It's about Finland. See here?" He jabbed a finger at a map showing the Soviet Union pressing against Finland.

"Last year, the Soviets—the Russians, you know, Communists—they tried to bully Finland. They demanded land and bases, just as they had with Lithuania, Latvia, and Estonia, and then took it. But Finland?" Darby's voice dropped to a conspiratorial whisper, his eyes wide.

"They actually told them no, Johnnie." Darby exclaimed. "Can you believe it? Little Finland stood up to the Ruskies!" He tapped a finger on a paragraph.

"Finland, Johnnie, it's a nation of four million strong, living off their forests and lakes. They've already fought off Communism and Fascism themselves, and they believe in laws and democracy. That's why America, Sweden, Norway, and Denmark—everyone is giving them support. Because Finland deserves it."

Darby's voice tightened, a fierce admiration hardening his gaze.

"Their lakes and vast swamps might stop Russian tanks in summer, but in winter, when everything freezes, it's perfect for ski troops. And Johnnie, the Finns are those ski troops! Just like Rolf told us about in Norway. They're dug in, they've got fortifications, and they're fighting."

He flipped to another page, the brittle paper crackling, showing stark black-and-white photos—blurred figures on skis, sleds pulled by reindeer, even men in white camouflage half-buried in snow, their faces grim but resolute.

Johnnie's finger traced the images while Darby went on—his voice hushed with awe. "See here—Carl Mydans, a Life Magazine photographer, was actually there," he exclaimed.

"He wrote about temperatures dropping to -45 degrees and how the Finns used reindeer to pull sleds and get around—because reindeer are silent and Russian tank fuel freezes. Ha! Their daily prayer was for snow and more cold!"

Darby paused and tried to lighten up. "They sure would love Lake Placid."

But then Darby's voice hardened, returning to his point.

"They're just this little country, but they stood up to the biggest bullies in Europe. Yeah, they ended up giving up some territory, but they fought so well that it made the world doubt Russia's military might. And, if that little country can do that to Russia—well, maybe someone will put a stop to Hitler. The world's changing, Johnnie. Bad people are doing bad things. And little countries, like Finland, are standing up to them, fighting for their freedom against a massive army, in the snow, in the cold."

Johnnie listened, the rhythmic splash of skipping stones fading into the background. The familiar world of Lake Placid —of hunting and ski patrol—suddenly felt small, distant, and almost irrelevant. The Lake, a vast, inky mirror, seemed to swallow the last embers of the sunset, its silence profound, broken only by the soft plink-plink-plink of skipping stones.

The idea of a small nation like Finland fighting back resonated deep within him, igniting a spark he hadn't known existed. He thought of his own life, armed with his simple slingshot, coaxing meals from the leanest woods, finding warmth where others shivered. This felt similar but bigger. A recognition of a purpose as clear as a mountain spring, a pull towards that clear line between right and wrong, a fight he knew, in his bones, he belonged to.

After a while and more skipping stones on the black Mirror Lake, a heavy silence settled between them, thick with the unsaid implications of Darby's words.

Johnnie's breath felt shallow in his lungs, the cold air suddenly sharper. Johnnie stared at the darkening water, the words forming slowly in his mind, then gaining an unstoppable momentum.

"Darby," he said, his voice low, almost a rumble in the deepening twilight, "I can't just sit here. The war's happening, over there. People are fighting for something important. I gotta go." The words felt urgent, a burning need having built up inside him for months.

Darby stopped stone mid-air, his hand frozen, his eyes wide with surprise and a sudden, sharp worry.

"Go where Johnnie?"

"Europe, to fight against Hitler with England. They're so desperate that they sometimes let younger guys in. I'm seventeen—I figure if I can get across, I can convince 'em."

Darby stared at him, the weight of the words settling like cold stones in his stomach. "Those doors are locked, Johnnie. FDR ran his whole reelection campaign on not getting the U.S. into the war. Volunteering to fight is effectively closed."

Johnnie's jaw was set, a familiar stubborn glint in his eye, reflecting the last embers of the sunset. "Then I'll try the back door," Johnnie said. "If Roosevelt won't let me fight, maybe Winston Churchill will. Canada is the back door to the war, and I intend to slip through it. I'm not deserting my country—just borrowing another's uniform. The war is calling, and Canada has left the back door open."

"But... my dad's going to get us into the Conservation Corps, Johnnie. And Rolf, he's counting on you for patrol this winter. He says nobody knows those peaks like you do. He needs you."

"I know," Johnnie said, his gaze fixed on the darkening water of the Lake, its currents a mirror of his restless spirit. "But this is bigger. This is... more real."

He didn't say goodbye, couldn't bring himself to utter the finality of the word.

Instead, he offered their old promise, a desperate hope for reunion: "See you at the top," before disappearing into the deepening twilight.

15

CANADA

The following day, in a cold, misty dawn, Darby searched everywhere—but Johnnie was gone. He went to the Olympic training facility and found Rolf; he would know what to do. "Rolf," Darby began, his voice a little shaky, the words catching in his throat. "It's Johnnie. He's gone. Said he was heading for Canada to join the war."

Rolf stopped, his hands still, the waxing iron cooling on the bench. A furrow appeared between his brows, deepening the lines of his weathered face, a shadow of concern.

He knew Johnnie's independent spirit, his restless desire for purpose, the burning fire of youth that sometimes outran common sense.

Without a word, he wiped his hands on a rag, grabbed his heavy coat, and motioned for Darby to follow, his movements quick and decisive.

They drove in Rolf's old pickup, the tires crunched rhythmically on the gravel roads, a steady counterpoint to the engine's hum.

As they went north to Canada, the air, thick with the mountain's mist, slowly burned off, revealing the familiar high peaks of the Adirondacks, painted with the first hints of autumn color —red, orange, yellow, green.

At the Canadian border crossing, a small, unassuming shack guarded by a single, bored-looking official, Rolf found Johnnie.

Johnnie sat hunched on the worn wooden bench, his shoulders slumped, the duffel bag beside him looking like a dead weight. Johnnie couldn't meet the official's eyes, a hot flush spreading across his cheeks, the fight drained from him.

"Didn't have the proper identification, did you, son?" the border official taunted, a hint of amusement playing on his lips. He leaned back in his chair, a slow, knowing smile spreading across his face, his gaze resting on Johnnie's embarrassed face.

Johnnie just nodded, unable to meet his eyes.

Rolf walked up, his quiet authority filling the small space. "He's with me," he told the official, his voice resonating with quiet command. "Just a boy with more courage than sense sometimes. We'll be heading back."

The official, recognizing Rolf, a local legend in his own right, simply waved them through, a small gesture of respect.

The drive back was largely silent. Johnnie expected a lecture, a furious scolding, a sharp rebuke for his foolishness. Still, Rolf said nothing, his gaze fixed on the winding road ahead.

Finally, as they pulled back into the familiar streets of Lake Placid and after they dropped off Darby at his house, Johnnie couldn't hold back.

"Are you angry, Rolf?" he asked, his voice barely a whisper, thick with shame.

Rolf pulled the truck to the side of the road and turned to face Johnnie. His eyes, typically sparkling with Nordic mischief, were serious now, reflecting a profound sadness and a distant pain.

For a fleeting moment, Rolf saw a flicker of snow-capped

mountains—not the Adirondacks, but a homeland under siege, a memory of friends and family living beneath a boot.

"Angry, Johnnie? How could I be angry?" He paused, a faraway look in his eyes.

"No one should ever be punished for doing something courageous, in the name of freedom. What you did, trying to fight the Germans, that was courageous. Foolish, perhaps, without the right papers," he added with a slight, softening smile, "but courageous nonetheless."

He continued, his voice softer now, imbued with quiet grief and a fierce, burning hope.

"I'm an American. But my old home country, Norway, is under German occupation. My friends, my family... they're living under that boot. I hope, one day, to join the US Army and go liberate them. To fight for them, just like you wanted to. So no, Johnnie. I could never be angry at a young man who feels that pull, that need to do what's right."

He clapped Johnnie on the shoulder, a firm, comforting pressure that spoke volumes.

"Our time will come. But when it does, it'll be on our terms, not theirs. And we'll be ready."

Johnnie looked at Rolf, a lump forming in his throat, his eyes stinging. He had expected anger, disappointment, and perhaps even a lecture about responsibility.

Instead, he found understanding and a shared, quiet resolve that bound them even tighter than before, a silent promise of a future fight.

He pledged then that when the time came, he would be ready.

16

THE CORPS

The year was 1940, and although the Great Depression was easing its grip, it still cast a long, dark shadow over the Adirondacks. Johnnie's sting of being turned away from enlisting in Canada because of his age was still fresh, a quiet frustration.

But, with Dr. Darby's connections, the Civilian Conservation Corps offered the boys another path—a way to serve, to move, to do something.

Johnnie and Darby, side by side since childhood, signed up for the CCC together and were sent to Camp S-71, a tent camp sprawling in a field near *The Whiteface Inn*, just west of their beloved Lake Placid and Mirror Lake.

Their days were long, beginning before dawn with the bugle's "rouse" call, a sharp, insistent sound that cut through the morning chill. The hours were filled with the rhythmic thud of axes, the scrape of shovels, and the clean, invigorating scent of pine sap that clung to their clothes and hair.

Camp life was demanding but familiar: early mornings, tools in hand, they would set out on an adventure to work in the woods, in the soil, instead of their old adventures playing guns in their neighbor's backyards.

They joined Company 218, where a dollar a day mainly went back home, and days passed in a rhythm of sweat, teamwork, and the scent of wood smoke.

Johnnie's hands, already calloused from chopping wood to heat the family cabin in his youth or fetching pails of clean, cool water from the stream out back, found that his hands grew even stronger in the Corps swinging axes, driving stakes and digging trails into the land he loved.

They planted long rows of red pines along the road between Ray Brook and Lake Placid, and when wildfires broke out—as they had savagely that year—they were among the enrollees who battled them. Faces streaked with ash, eyes stinging from smoke, they pressed on with quiet resolve, moving in practiced patterns, shoulders squared.

However, it wasn't just about planting trees and fighting fires. The Corps was building the very infrastructure of the Adirondacks, connecting isolated communities and opening up the untouched wilderness to the world.

They helped construct trails that snaked through the wild beauty, roads that opened up new vistas, and campsites where families would one day gather under the stars.

Johnnie and Darby, still just boys in some ways, learned to work with a team, to trust their fellow man with their lives in dangerous situations, and to see the tangible results of their labor transforming the land before their eyes.

The mountains, which had always been in Johnnie's bones, were now being shaped by his hands alongside his oldest friend, forging a connection deeper than ever before.

And then came word from afar: the 1940 Olympics—once a dream on the horizon for their friend Rolf—had been canceled.

The war in Europe was expanding. The world was shifting, and they could feel it in the wind.

17

WHITEFACE MOUNTAIN

It was a steamy July morning when the call came: forty CCC boys were needed to help complete a vital telephone line to the summit of Whiteface Mountain. Though technically from Camp S-71, Johnnie and Darby were temporarily assigned to Camp S-90. Transfers like that weren't unusual, especially for hard workers with a growing reputation for grit and reliability.

They packed light—just essentials—and headed out, ready for something new. This job was different.

At Whiteface's higher elevations, the soft earth gave way to unforgiving granite. Wooden poles cracked and splintered under the stress of wind and exposure. Only steel would do.

Their mission was to drill deep into the rock, setting steel anchor poles for a line that would run from the mountain's base to the fire tower on its summit.

The labor was grueling. The sun glared off the pale rock, and the air thinned with each foot of elevation. But there was no other way.

Johnnie, with his instinct for terrain, often picked the best anchor points. He could sense the rock's strengths, where it would hold, and where it might give. Darby, meticulous as ever, focused on precision—every bolt, every bore, exact.

The sound of steel striking stone rang out constantly, echoing down the slopes like the mountain's own heartbeat.

The goal was clear: to give the fire ranger atop Whiteface a dependable line—one that could transmit a call through storm, fire, or worse. It was more than a construction job. It was a lifeline, stretched thin and strong through the vast Adirondack wild.

18

HOTLINE

Through August heat and mountain storms, the line slowly climbed. Day after day, the CCC boys pushed the cable higher—mile after mile, pole after pole. From Cone's Camp on Lake Placid to the summit tower, the steel spine grew, each section linked by blistered hands and sweat-soaked shirts.

It was punishing work—hauling cable over granite, straining against the slope, driving bolts into unforgiving stone—but they were determined. Every twist of wire was deliberate. Every lash of the line held meaning. This wasn't just about telephone service. It was about proving they could do something that mattered.

Then, finally, the line was ready.

One hot afternoon, the foreman gave a sharp nod. Johnnie stood nearby, sweat streaking down his face, his shirt clinging to his back. They watched as a pulse of electricity shot through the line.

A soft crackle buzzed from the ranger's telephone receiver.

Then, a voice. Distant—but clear.

They'd done it. A lifeline, built to survive the harsh mountain environment, now climbed the mountain.

Johnnie didn't say much; he just smiled at Darby, who smiled back.

19

THE WILMINGTON TRAIL

When it came time for Darby to re-enlist in the CCC, his father intervened. Dr. Darby, determined to steer his son toward a different future, insisted that he focus on academics. "No more CCC, Edgar," he'd said, his voice firm. "You're going to college. I've arranged for a tutor in town; you'll study for your entrance exams."

Darby, while understanding his father's intentions, felt a pang of regret.

Johnnie, who had never even dreamed of college, didn't quite grasp the significance of Darby's new path. Still, he understood the quiet resignation in his friend's eyes.

Without Darby by his side, Johnnie decided to re-enlist with Camp S-90, located closer to Whiteface Mountain, where a new project was underway: building the first hiking trail up the imposing peak.

Here, he met foremen and engineers from the US Geological Survey (USGS), men who carried rolls of intricate topographic maps and spoke a language of contours and elevations.

They took Johnnie under their wing, teaching him how to

read complex maps, evaluate a mountain's slope gradients, identify natural ridgelines, understand water drainage patterns, and pinpoint crucial rock outcrops and ledges.

This knowledge was essential for picking the best route to bushwhack and building a sustainable path to the summit.

Johnnie felt a deeper connection to their work. These weren't just narrow paths they carved through the wilderness; they were promises, a silent language shared between the mountain and those who sought its heights.

Every careful observation and every chosen route felt like etching a lasting direction into the land itself, a distinct guide for those who would follow.

They routed trails along ridges, minimizing erosion and providing hikers with better footing. They meticulously followed the thousand-year-old paths used by deer and bears.

These animals instinctively identified the most practical routes that minimized steep grades and included natural switchbacks, often leading to the wild blueberries that blossomed each spring on the mountaintop, a testament to the efficiency of nature's design.

Johnnie, with his innate understanding of the wilderness, excelled at this. He led small teams on reconnaissance hikes, confirming the proposed paths and often suggesting changes to ensure hikers could enjoy the most scenic views at lookouts on the way to the summit.

He proudly led the final team that painted the trail marks: 2-inch by 6-inch blue blazes on trees spaced every 100 to 200 feet along the new trail.

Every mark was a clear, silent guide for those who would follow.

He understood, even then, that some marks were more than just paint on a tree; they were promises to others of safe passage.

Johnnie never felt prouder than when they commissioned

the 7.4-mile "Wilmington Trail," as it was named, with a ribbon-cutting ceremony.

It was the first official hiking trail to Whiteface's imposing 4,867-foot summit, a tangible legacy etched into the very rock of the Adirondacks.

THE LAKE PLACID NEWS

January 10, 1941

Ski Soldiers Have Anti-Tank, Machine Guns Here With Them

A new contingent of 26th U.S. Infantry ski troops started training at Placid this week and may be seen in action on the slopes and trails each day under Rolf Monsen, instructor. This week's soldier group has been augmented by a special detachment, all of which are completely equipped with combat equipment, consisting of packs, rifles, side arms, machine and anti-tank guns for actual winter war maneuvers under snow conditions.

Machine guns will be mounted on dog-sleds and toboggans and will be drawn into battle position by sled dogs, while others will be packed into position by troops and assembled on the firing line. Anti-tank guns, mounted on skis, will be drawn over roads, trails and slopes by a sno-mobile as an experiment with this type of transportation. Colonel C. A. Lundy has been assigned to the detachment to study various types of transportation and training that might be effectively utilized by the army in defending parts of the country in which snow would be a serious factor.

This is the first of a series of experiments that will be carried out by the 26th Infantry here during the winter. The regiment, which will form the nucleus of the First U.S. Winter Combat division, is under the command of Colonel James I. Muir, with barracks at the town hall with new men assigned each week for ski training.

20

A SHADOW OVER THE SUMMIT

The world was changing, and even in the Adirondacks, the distant rumblings of war grew louder. Johnnie, now eighteen, continued his double life—a Civilian Conservation Corps enrollee by weekday and a dedicated National Ski Patroller by weekend. The skills he honed, seemingly for conservation and rescue, were unknowingly preparing him for a far more significant challenge—a destiny stretching beyond the peaceful valleys of his home.

He and Darby would occasionally talk about the war, their voices low as they sat around a crackling fire in the warming hut after a long day on patrol. They'd heard stories, fragmented and grim, of the brutal fighting in Europe, the immense courage of soldiers facing unimaginable odds, the devastation wrought upon ancient cities.

Johnnie, who had tried to enlist in Canada at seventeen and been turned away, the sting of that rejection still a quiet ache, felt a growing sense of anticipation, a feeling that his unique talents, his profound connection to the mountains, might be needed for something more, for a fight far more significant than any wildfire or rescue mission.

The stage was being set, though Johnnie didn't know it, for a letter that would irrevocably alter his path, leading him far from the familiar peaks of the Adirondacks into the heart of the coming storm: the formation of the 10th Mountain Division and the call for ski patrollers like him.

THE LAKE PLACID NEWS

December 7, 1941

Pearl Harbor Attack: Local Boys Affected

21

THE LETTER

The snow was falling, a soft, hushed blanket covering the world in pristine white the morning Johnnie pulled the envelope from the rusted mailbox outside his family's cabin. The metal was cold beneath his fingers, the small flag on the box stiff with frost.

The letter was stamped with an official seal, sharp and clear against the white paper, and addressed in a neat, deliberate hand: *From Charles Minot Dole, National Ski Patrol Headquarters.* The name, infamous among the ski community, now stood boldly on the envelope addressed to Johnnie. He tore it open with cold, bare hands, the paper crackling in the frigid air, the sound loud in the quiet morning.

To the men of the Ski Patrol:

The War Department is actively seeking skilled mountaineers and skiers for a new, specialized combat unit, the 10th Mountain Division, being formed to operate in mountainous and winter conditions. You have been recognized as one of the most qualified for such a role. Details regarding the unit's designation and formal activation will follow;

however, we appreciate your early commitment. If you are willing to serve your country in this capacity, please respond by return mail.

You will be tested beyond anything you've known—at altitude, on ice, in silence and snow. But you were born for this.

—Charles Minot Dole, Director of the National Ski Patrol (NSP)

Johnnie stood still, allowing the snow to accumulate on his shoulders, which dissolved into cold dampness unnoticed. The words on the page seemed to sear, imprinting themselves directly onto his mind. It wasn't a command, nor was it a mandatory enlistment. It was an invitation—a summons into history itself, a call to a purpose he had felt stirring within him for years.

He wasn't alone. The same letter, identical in its blunt message and profound implications, was part of a direct appeal from Minot Dole himself. Dole launched a mass letter-writing campaign aimed at reaching nearly every member of the National Ski Patrol—men who understood the deadly secrets of avalanches—a terrifying force of nature that had been weaponized with lethal effect to sabotage and kill soldiers in World War I—and the intricacies of skiing, snowshoeing, and climbing up sheer ice cliffs.

These were men who could intuitively read the coming weather in the whisper of the trees and deeply understood the silent, often perilous, language of the high places. From seasoned veterans to eager young men alike, the response was nearly universal, communicated in the same simple, unwavering answer:

Yes.

Johnnie didn't hesitate. The decision felt less like a choice and more like an inevitability. He penned his reply at the kitchen table that night, the fire casting a warm, intimate glow on his determined face, illuminating the quiet resolve in his eyes.

> Mr. Dole,
>
> I accept.
>
> —Johnnie Grey, Lake Placid Ski Patrol

By the time he sealed the envelope, his hands were trembling—not from the cold, but from something deeper, a tremor of anticipation and a profound sense of destiny.

The trail ahead was uncertain, shrouded in the mists of war, leading away from the familiar comfort of the Adirondacks and into the unknown. But he knew this much, with a certainty that settled deep in his bones:

He had been called, and he would climb.

22

A DIFFERENT PATH

The crisp Adirondack air, usually a balm, felt heavy with unspoken futures as Johnnie made his way to Darby's grand house. The letter from Minot Dole, a burning summons to the mountains of war, was tucked inside his jacket, its direct words echoing in his mind.

He found Darby in the study, surrounded by books. The scent of old paper and polished wood filled the room, creating a stark contrast to the wood-smoke-scented world of Johnnie.

"Darby," Johnnie began, his voice low and trembling with anticipation. He pulled out the letter, its official seal a stark declaration: "You got one of these, didn't you? It's happening. We're going."

He didn't ask if Darby was going; it was an unspoken assumption, a shared destiny forged in snow-fights and mountain climbs.

Darby's gaze, usually so quick and bright, was shadowed. He nodded slowly; a similar envelope lay freshly opened. "Johnnie, I got the letter, but I'm not going." He took a breath and said, "It's my dad and West Point."

Johnnie's brow furrowed. "West Point? What about it?"

Darby sighed, running a hand through his hair. "He's pulling every string he has. He was a doctor in the trenches in the Great War, Johnnie. He saw... things. Things that twisted men and broke their spirits. He calls it 'Hell,' and the way he says it, Johnnie, it's a word scorched into his soul. He just... he wants to delay his only son being sent into that."

A silence fell between them, thick with the weight of diverging paths. Johnnie understood.

His father, Mr. Sandford's distant weariness, and the clank of his prosthetic hand served as quiet indicators of a war Johnnie couldn't yet comprehend. Now, the silent horrors Mr. Sandford carried began to take shape in Johnnie's mind.

"I get it," Johnnie finally said, the words tasting sour.

He had nothing but love for Dr. Darby, and he would do anything that man asked of him. Johnnie swallowed, the words 'I get it' feeling hollow.

He stood, a heavy silence settling between them, the unspoken farewell a physical weight in the room.

As Johnnie walked out the front door and down the wide, sweeping porch, the autumn leaves crunching under his boots, a sudden shout cut through the quiet.

"Hey, Johnnie!"

Darby was at the edge of the porch, his voice raw with a mixture of longing and fierce loyalty.

Johnnie stopped, turning back, a tired but resolute grin spreading across his face. The words, their old childhood challenge, now carried a new, profound meaning.

Johnnie yelled, "I'll see you at the top!" his voice carrying on the crisp, cold air, a promise whispered to the mountains.

Darby, a pained smile touching his lips, called back, "Not if I get there first!"

23

PLAYING GUNS

As Johnnie rode his rusty, patched bike home—a hand-made, pieced-together machine—the ache in his chest was a dull counterpoint to the sharp sting of Dr. Darby's words.

Saying goodbye to his mom, Allee, and Darby—who, he knew, would ace his exams and get into West Point—was hard enough. But the doctor's anger, his harsh candor about The Great War, kept circling in Johnnie's mind, a confusing breach of what Johnnie had always believed to be taboo.

When they were younger, Johnnie, Darby, and the other boys played "guns," imagining themselves as soldiers in World War I. Ironically, the fathers who had fought never spoke of it; only the medals tucked away or visible injuries like Mr. Sandford's served as reminders.

Johnnie instinctively knew it was taboo to ask adults about World War I. The unspoken scars, the lingering coughs, and the haunted eyes made the subject too heavy, too real.

He had always believed it forbidden for adults to speak ill of the war, an unspoken pact where boys played their games and fathers kept their silence.

Now, with the taboo shattered, a fierce need ignited in Johnnie: to finally learn what had happened to his father.

ENLISTED AS A PRIVATE (PVT.)

September 1942

From seasoned veterans to eager young men, the response to the plea from Minnie Dole, Director of the National Ski Patrol, was extraordinary. Nearly all those contacted—all civilian volunteers—agreed to serve in some capacity. The NSP then undertook the critical task of vetting thousands of applications. One of these was Johnnie Grey, who quickly passed the vetting process and met the rigorous requirements.

Private Johnnie Grey enlisted in the U.S. Army on 17 September 1942, and was later re-assigned to the newly formed 86th Mountain Infantry Regiment of the 10th Mountain Division. In total, the NSP vetted and recruited about 10,000 of the 14,000 men into the 10th Mountain Division, establishing the experienced backbone of its specialized fighting force.

24

SNOW AND ALTITUDE

Winter 1942-1943

Johnnie was nineteen years old, his frame lean and hardened by years of mountain living and CCC labor, and he was ready. He joined the newly formed 10th Mountain Division, trading the familiar peaks of the Adirondacks for the formidable, towering ranges of the Colorado Rockies.

His basic training ground: Camp Hale, a place as wild and unforgiving as his home, but with a sharp, military precision.

Camp Hale sat high in the Colorado Rockies, a vast, desolate expanse wrapped in snow and a silence that was often broken. The wind howled between the barracks, a mournful, constant presence, or the dull thud of artillery echoed across the valley, a low, guttural growl that served as a constant reminder of their purpose.

At an altitude of 9,200 feet, every breath felt like a chore, thin and sharp, burning in his lungs. The altitude punished lungs and knees alike, separating the merely strong from the truly resilient, testing every man who dared to set foot there.

The train, a long, dark serpent of olive-drab passenger cars, the stale air inside thick with the collective breath of anxious young men, the smell of sweat, and faint diesel fumes, its windows grimy from the long, rattling journey, had barely pulled into the makeshift station when a Sergeant's bellow, raw and powerful, cut through the wind: "Out! Grab your rucks, move!"

Johnnie arrived in the teeth of a snowstorm, the flakes like stinging needles against his face, blurring the world into a chaotic white. The air stung his face, but a broad, exhilarated grin stretched across his lips, reflecting genuine joy. This was it. This was where he belonged.

Johnnie quickly found his bunk in the barracks, a sea of identical double-decker cots. Their rucksacks, weighing a good ninety pounds with all their gear, were stowed beneath.

His bunkmate was Mineo, a short guy from Connecticut. Next to them in the corner were Hogan and Luby, two city boys from Albany and Menands, NY. They quickly bonded over shared exhaustion and the sheer absurdity of their new lives.

In January 1943, after his exceptional performance during initial training, Johnnie was called before his commanding officer. "Grey," the Sergeant said, a flicker of respect in his eyes, "your file says you were born on skis. Looks like it's true. Congratulations, Private First Class." He handed Johnnie the new stripes, a small but significant recognition of the skills he'd brought with him.

That night, the barracks were quiet except for the low whistle of the wind and the rhythmic sound of men cleaning their gear. The promotion felt good, but it also felt distant, a small thing in a vast, cold place. Johnnie sat on his bunk, oiling the bolt of his M1, when Hogan let out a frustrated sigh from the corner.

"I swear, my father could take this rifle apart and put it back together blindfolded in under a minute," Hogan muttered, struggling with a stubborn pin. "He was a machinist at the armory. Said if a man can't maintain his tools, he's no man at all. I'm pretty sure he respects his rifles more than he respects me." He finally forced the pin free with a grunt. "I just... I gotta show him I can handle this."

Mineo looked up from the letter he was writing. "My old man runs a tailor shop in Hartford. All day long, it's suits and fine fabrics." He gestured around the barracks with his pen. "He wanted me to take over the business. Said a man's hands are for creating, not destroying. I told him someone's gotta make sure it's safe for guys like him to run tailor shops. That's what we're doing here." He folded the letter carefully. "Still, I hope he understands."

Listening to them, Johnnie felt a familiar, hollow pang of envy. He wished his father was alive, not just so he could join the conversation, but so he could have a man like that to measure up to. He looked at them—Hogan, fighting for his father's respect, and Mineo, fighting for a principle his father couldn't see. He knew that weight.

For years, his own burden had been for his Mom and Allee. Now, looking at his new brothers-in-arms, he felt that responsibility expand—an unspoken promise to see them through whatever was coming.

25

THE POWDER TRAP

After basic training, the ski drills began. The instructors, hardened mountaineers themselves and veterans of countless slopes and unforgiving conditions, expected to spend the first few days teaching the recruits, such as Hogan, Mineo, and Luby, who were not ski patrol trained, how to stand without falling and how to descend a mild slope without turning into a human snowball.

But when Johnnie stepped into his skis, it was like watching a hawk stretch its wings, ready for effortless flight. He moved with the mountain, not against it, a natural extension of the landscape. Graceful. Effortless. Precise. His movements were a silent poem of motion.

"Where did you learn to ski like that, PFC Grey?" one instructor asked, squinting against the blinding glare of the sun on snow, his voice filled with genuine surprise and a hint of awe. "Lake Placid," Johnnie replied, his voice calm, his gaze steady. “Rolf Monsen taught me." The man whistled low, a sound of understanding and respect. “That explains it."

One afternoon, during an intense powder training run, Mineo, usually nimble, hit a patch of unseen ice. He flailed wildly for a moment, let out a surprised yell, and then disappeared over the edge of a cliff. Johnnie, Hogan, and Luby skied frantically to the edge, their hearts in their throats.

"Mineo! Mineo!" they all yelled, their voices echoing in the vast, silent expanse of snow. No answer. Just the whisper of the wind.

"He's gone," Hogan whispered, his face pale. "Poof."

"Well," Luby muttered, already unstrapping his skis, "someone's gotta go down there and see if there's anything left to bury." The men just stared at him quizzically, as they always did, trying to figure out if he was being serious.

Just as they were about to begin their grim descent, Mineo's muffled shout, seemingly from the very depths of the snow, reached them. "Hey! Help!"

They peered over the edge to see Mineo buried in a massive, fluffy snowdrift, completely unharmed. His head had just popped out of the drift, and he was grinning from ear to ear—happy to be alive.

He'd fallen into a hidden snow pocket, a deep, soft cushion of powder. The relief that washed over them was immediate and overwhelming, quickly giving way to shouts of laughter.

Hogan pushed Luby off the edge, and he landed next to Mineo. So Johnnie pushed Hogan off the edge, who landed with a soft thump behind them. The three of them mimicked kids making snow angels.

"Look out Hitler." Luby grinned. "Here come the snow angels." They all laughed.

26

D-SERIES

The crisp, high-altitude air of Camp Hale became a brutal adversary when the divisional maneuvers, called D-Series, began in the winter of 1943, transforming the sprawling training ground into a crucible of ice and unrelenting cold.

This was no longer just about skiing and climbing; it was about surviving out in the field against the elements, serving as a tactical proving ground.

Johnnie, Mineo, Hogan, and Luby, along with their fellow recruits, were plunged into conditions designed to mimic the unforgiving Italian Apennines, forbidden from building open fires in sub-zero temperatures, even when off duty.

They slept in canvas tents, and throughout the night, the moisture in their breath would create frost on the inside top of the tent. The wind, a constant, mournful presence, howled through the tent flaps and across the desolate expanse of snow, its biting breath a physical torment.

One afternoon, as they pushed through a particularly exposed ridge, the sun, a cold, indifferent eye in the pale sky, offered little warmth despite the thermometer hovering high that day, around 32 degrees.

Hogan, his face already a mottled red, his lips blue, shivered violently, his teeth chattering uncontrollably. "H-h-how c-can I b-be s-s-so c-cold on a w-w-warm and s-s-sunny 32-degree d-day?" he stammered, his voice thin and reedy against the wind.

Johnnie, whose face, though drawn with fatigue, showed less of the raw, exposed agony of the others, knelt, pulling Hogan's balaclava higher over his cheeks. "It's what we call a 'wind chill' back on the top of Whiteface Mountain," Johnnie explained, his voice low but clear.

"Doesn't matter if it's sunny and 32 degrees. If the wind is blowing a steady 40 miles per hour up here in the mountains, that 32 degrees feels like it's 13 degrees. You can get frostbite without even knowing it's happening."

He gestured to his face, which was almost entirely covered by a scarf and the hood of his parka. "The only way to protect yourself is to cover every exposed bit of skin."

He then began to meticulously adjust their gear, pulling Mineo's scarf tighter around his neck, ensuring Luby's ear flaps were fully deployed, and even tearing strips from a spare piece of cloth to fashion makeshift face coverings for those whose skin was most exposed.

He showed how to tuck sleeves into gloves, check for blanching skin, and maintain circulation even while resting.

"Where in God's name did you learn all this, Johnnie?" Mineo mumbled, his eyes wide with a newfound respect. The cold forced a quiet humility into his usual confident demeanor.

"Part of ski patrol training back home," Johnnie replied, his voice flat, his mind briefly flashing back to Rolf Monsen's stern lessons on avalanche awareness and rescue protocol, now suddenly, chillingly relevant. "You can't save anyone if you get yourself killed in the process first."

They all nodded as if this was news to them.

On all maneuvers, Johnnie was now leading the pack on every timed descent, executing perfect turns that left clean, sharp lines in the snow. He navigated the uphill switchbacks with the efficiency of a seasoned Olympian, his movements precise and economical.

Even the officers, usually detached and focused on their duties, took notice of his natural talent, a raw, undeniable gift.

But it wasn't just speed. It was how Johnnie made it look easy and quietly helped others improve with humility and without showing off. He'd stop on a slope, patient and observant, point out their mistakes with a quiet word, then demonstrate a smoother, more efficient way down, his body a living example.

The men respected him for it, recognizing his quiet strength and genuine willingness to help.

By now, he was outperforming even the instructors on tactical war runs, his endurance seemingly limitless, his understanding of the snow and terrain almost supernatural.

The D-Series maneuvers were relentless, a grueling test that lasted weeks. They were tactical war games designed to forge hardened mountain soldiers, but the cost was evident.

By the end, the division saw 195 cases of frostbite and 340 other incapacitating injuries, a grim testament to the extreme nature of the training.

Johnnie and his squad of twelve soldiers, though battered and exhausted, returned to Camp Hale alive and intact, their bodies aching, their minds reeling, but their bond cemented by shared hardship.

They were among the survivors, a testament to Johnnie's quiet leadership and the unforgiving lessons of the Adirondack Mountains.

~

THE DAY they returned to the main barracks in May 1943, their platoon leader pulled Johnnie aside. "Grey, what you did out there... keeping your men's heads straight, teaching them about wind chill... that was leadership. The brass noticed." He pressed a set of Corporal stripes into Johnnie's hand. "These are earned. Don't let me down."

27

FEATHERS

Having survived D-Series, a small group of them, including Johnnie, Mineo, Hogan, and Luby, got a weekend pass and hitchhiked on the back of a truck into the nearest town. This small, dusty outpost seemed more like a tumbleweed than a civilization.

As they hopped into the back of the truck, another soldier who was sitting and catching a ride into town said hello and yelled, "What's your name?" over the roar of the wind as the truck picked up speed.

Luby responded, "Luby," and the soldier affirmed, "Yes." To which Luby puzzled, "Yes, What?" and the soldier repeated, "Luby." Now, Luby was ordinarily a pretty tolerant guy. Still, it was becoming apparent that the soldier in the back of the truck was mocking him in some way.

Johnnie tried to intercede, pointed to Luby, and said, "That's Luby - what's your name, soldier?"

The soldier looked back and forth, now confused, thinking they were playing a prank on him. He replied, "No, I'm Luby." At this point, Hogan and Mineo were cracking up because they had figured it out - they both turned to each other and yelled, "There are two Luby's!"

Mineo asked the soldier, "What's your full name?" He replied, "Bob Luby." Mineo pointed his thumb and clarified, "Our Luby is named John Luby."

John and Bob Luby shook hands and spent the rest of the trip sharing stories about their families and their Irish roots. Turns out there is a town in Ireland called "Bally Luby."

Upon hearing this, Mineo and Hogan's faces lit up again as they both made another realization at the same time, but Hogan shouted it out first: "There's a whole valley of Luby's somewhere!"

Together, the two Lubys, Johnnie, Mineo, and Hogan found a saloon.

Its interior was surprisingly warm and crowded, almost filled with other soldiers, their laughter and shouts echoing off the rough-hewn walls. They nursed a few Coors, the taste surprisingly potent at 9,200 feet. They swapped stories of home and the bizarre realities of mountain warfare training. Then, the new Luby met up with his squad and left them.

By the time they caught a ride back to Camp Hale, they were feeling the effects of the alcohol, each step a little less steady, each laugh a little louder. The thin mountain air only amplified the tipsiness. They stumbled into the barracks, collapsing onto their cots with exaggerated sighs of contentment.

That night, around 1:00 a.m., a yell emanated from Hogan and Luby's corner of the barracks - "Help! Help!"

The shrieking voice sounded like the voice of a cartoon character being strangled.

Johnnie and Mineo woke and ran to Hogan and Luby's bunk through what appeared to be snow in the barrack's air and all over the cold cement floor.

As they got closer to Hogan, the snow got thicker, and they

saw him sitting up. Luby was striking Hogan repeatedly on his back.

Luby tells them, “I’m trying to dislodge it.”

Hogan keeps screeching. "Help! Help!” his voice comically muffled. "There's a feather in my throat!”

Hogan was one of the lucky ones who had a down sleeping bag, but it had ruptured earlier in the night, releasing most of its fluffy white contents into the air as he tossed and turned through the night.

Johnnie and Mineo looked at each other, then at the feather-covered Hogan, and burst out laughing.

Mineo tossed Hogan a canteen of water so he could wash the feather down his throat.

28

THE ROCKS

Summer 1943

The next day, a jeep, churning up dust and kicking up a cloud of suspicion, arrived at the command tent at the base of the hiking trail. A tall, angular officer, his uniform crisp despite the conditions, stepped out and spoke in hushed tones to the head of the skiing unit.

Papers were exchanged in a brief, silent manner, and heads nodded in agreement. Ten minutes later, Johnnie was called into the tent, a vague sense of unease settling in his stomach, a premonition.

"You're being reassigned, Corporal Grey," the officer said, his tone clipped and efficient.

"Sir?" Johnnie asked, surprise coloring his voice, his brow furrowing.

"Climbing school. Seneca Rocks, West Virginia. You'll leave tomorrow." While Johnnie was shocked, and didn't want to leave his new friends, he automatically replied, "Yes, Sir."

The officer looked at him, a rare, genuine smile touching

his lips, a flash of warmth in his stern face. "You're too good to keep on the ground Grey. Let's see if you can climb like you ski."

Johnnie saluted, the crisp movement automatic, and returned to pack his ruck, his mind already turning to the new challenge.

As he glanced back at the snow-capped peaks of Camp Hale, the raw, beautiful challenge of them, he felt a flicker of pride, a quiet satisfaction.

He'd proved himself here. Now, it was time to climb.

29

THE CLIFFS

Summer 1943

Corporal Johnnie Grey arrived at Seneca Rocks along with 31 men, many of them seasoned instructors, a hard-bitten group plucked from the unforgiving peaks of Colorado. The air was thick and heavy with the haze of a humid Appalachian summer, markedly different from the crisp, thin air of Camp Hale's high-altitude training grounds.

Their assignment, simple on paper, was anything but easy: establish a low-altitude climbing school, a crucible for the next generation of mountain soldiers, at the Seneca Rocks formations, nestled on the south branch of the Potomac River.

Johnnie's extensive experience from his time in the Civilian Conservation Corps, particularly his innate understanding of terrain, outdoor construction, and sustained physical labor, proved invaluable from day one—a fact that many of the veteran instructors quickly noted and appreciated.

They immediately set about building wooden buildings and pitching canvas tents, transforming the rugged landscape into a functional training camp.

To further hone essential techniques before soldiers moved on to actual rock formations, such as Seneca Rocks itself, they first built sturdy 20-foot-tall wooden climbing towers.

These structures, designed for practicing foundational rope work, including knot tying, belaying, and rappelling, as well as various other climbing techniques, quickly earned a nickname from the farm boys: "corn cribs," a name that resonated with many of the soldier's agricultural roots and stuck.

With the base camp and the corn crib climbing towers built, they then moved to the imposing quartzite Rockwall blade itself, where they meticulously mapped different ascents up the 900-foot face, identifying routes that would challenge and prepare their future trainees.

Crucially, the instructors free-climbed the Rockwall to install robust rope installations that would allow instructors to be side by side with the trainees as they made their way up the sheer faces, guiding them through the daunting process of driving pitons into the rock for the very first time—a fundamental skill for creating secure anchor points in mountain warfare.

When the oppressive heat of the summer sun became unbearable, they would seek brief, welcome respite by swimming in the calm, refreshing, muddy waters of the Potomac River, washing away the dust and sweat of the day.

30

THE CRUCIBLE

Once the base was complete, Johnnie underwent his own intensive climbing training program at Seneca Rocks. The program was designed to change a soldier forever, to strip away the softness and forge something harder, more resilient, something capable of facing the impossible.

Day One began with names on a roster and ended with scraped knuckles, blistered palms, and bone-deep exhaustion that settled into Johnnie's very marrow. Each morning started before the sun, the mountain still shrouded in a pre-dawn gloom, the air cool and damp.

Reveille echoed through the hollow, sharp and insistent. By first light, they tied knots by lantern glow. Their fingers fumbled at first, then slowly, painstakingly found their rhythm. Each loop and twist became second nature.

Johnnie adapted quickly; his Adirondack sense of the mountains proved accurate. However, the Appalachian quartzite, with its slick and brittle texture, required more precise footwork and firmer grips, presenting him with a new kind of puzzle to solve.

He got the hang of the figure-eight, the bowline, and the clove hitch—the very knots a man needed to tie off his rope and make sure he and the mountain were joined correctly.

Each knot was a quiet pledge, a link in a chain, showing what a man could rely on and trust. The rope itself became his lifeline—a path to safety and a helping hand.

He put his mind to remembering every anchor point, figuring out how to use what nature provided—a sturdy tree, a big rock—or, if need be, driving steel pitons into the rock cracks with a hammer when nothing else would hold.

Belaying was a plain affair—usually a hip belay, where the rope was wrapped around the man's own body to make it bite and hold. There were no gadgets or machines for it; it was all in how you stood, how tight you held, and the skill of your hands.

They drilled belaying in pairs: one man climbing, the other holding the rope, both fastened to either end of a stout hemp line. The anchors were simple enough—steel pitons hammered into the rock, the rope either clipped through a metal ring called a carabiner or just run straight through.

Sometimes, a man would pretend to fall from the top of a corn crib, and the belayer, digging his heels in or bracing against a solid point, would use his hip to stop the drop. It was rough on the hands and gave no quarter, but it held—if you knew your business.

Johnnie got the hang of keeping his partner safe, knowing just when to let the rope run free and when to tighten it down. He learned to trust the feel of the rope in his hands, sensing the pull and give before his eyes could even see it.

Then came the grips for hands and feet—the tricky, risky business of putting your life in the hands of rough stone, finding a solid grip or foothold where there seemed to be none, and holding on to the straight-up world.

They clawed their way up sheer rock faces in small groups of three, the instructors shouting advice and curses in equal measure, their voices bouncing off the stone, driving the men beyond what they thought they could do.

Then came rappelling—a head-spinning drop, a way to get down a rope using only the rope itself and the rub against your own body.

There were no newfangled gadgets for this; Johnnie's first time down was done Dülfersitz-style—the rope laid across one shoulder, down his back, and around the other thigh. Only the friction of the rope around his body and his strength would keep him from falling to his death.

His gut clenched as he backed off the edge, but once his boots hit the ground and the rope went loose, a powerful surge went through him. He wanted to do it again—to beat the fear, to master the drop, to feel that power of being in charge.

Their lead instructor was Technical Sergeant Miles McCaffrey—a wiry, deep-voiced veteran from Montana who seemed carved from stone himself, his face a roadmap of hard-won experience, his eyes sharp and unforgiving. He greeted the men at Seneca Rocks with a gravelly snarl: "You don't get to pick your weather in a war, boys." McCaffrey growled. "Rain, sleet, snow—the enemy doesn't care. And neither do I."

They climbed in driving rain that bit at their exposed skin, that turned the rock treacherous and slick, under a blazing sun that sapped their strength and left them parched.

McCaffrey pushed them to exhaustion beyond what they thought their bodies could endure, past the point of pain into a realm of pure will. Blisters turned to calluses, then to hardened scars, each one a mark of their progress.

A few, unable to meet the brutal demands, washed out, their bags packed, and sent back to Camp Hale.

The rest learned to move like goats on vertical cliffs; every movement was precise and efficient. Their fear transmuted into focus, and their bodies became extensions of the rock.

Over time, their confidence grew—too much for Tech Sergeant McCaffrey's taste.

One morning, as the metallic ring of steel against stone echoed too loudly through the hollow, a jarring sound that would betray their presence, he growled, his voice a low, dangerous rumble, "You want the whole Nazi army to know you're here? From now on, we climb quiet."

His eyes were like flint, boring into them. "From now on, I better not hear your gear. Not a clink. Not a whisper. You move like shadows."

They had to relearn everything, shedding recently mastered instincts and habits.

They hammered pitons with muffled, short, deliberate strokes, wrapping hammers in cloth or leather and gripping the mallet head for precise, controlled taps.

Communication shifted to hand signals, an unspoken sign language replacing their voices.

Each exhalation was a controlled effort, a silent discipline, as they breathed through clenched jaws. To minimize clinking, they taped their metal gear, tying down every piece to avoid betraying sounds.

McCaffrey made them climb at night, moving up the rock in silence, with only the darkness and indifferent stars as witnesses.

It was a maddening, brutal reeducation, but it proved effective. Johnnie learned to read stone in the pitch black with his fingers as his eyes, tracing subtle veins and fissures for the slightest grip.

His initial apprehension and fear faded, replaced by unwavering skill, quiet confidence, and deep trust in his body and the rock itself. He learned the unyielding truth of adherence, the vital importance of an unwavering grip when all else threatened to give way.

It was war, in rehearsal, with the unforgiving rocks as judge and jury, determining who would survive and who would fall.

At the very end of his intensive training in October 1943, Johnnie was summoned to the mess tent. When he entered, all the men, including the instructors, stood and began to clap.

In an impromptu ceremony, McCaffrey held up a set of Sergeant stripes. "You don't just know how to climb, Grey," he growled, a rare hint of a smile on his face. "You know how to lead men up a rock."

He pressed the cloth chevrons firmly into Johnnie's hand. "Get these sewn on. You've earned them."

McCaffrey then grinned. "And as a new instructor, you get one other perk: 'Only instructors and staff can go into town on the weekends.'" The Army, he explained, kept trainees confined to base.

31

THE FIRST WEEKEND

After weeks of grueling training, the instructors were granted their first-weekend pass, a taste of freedom after endless days of rock and discipline.

Johnnie and a few buddies made their way into Elkins, the nearest town, catching a ride on a supply truck with the promise of a diner, a blue plate special, a movie theater showing the latest Western, and, most enticingly, a Friday night dance at the Grange Hall. The journey itself felt like an escape, the dusty road a ribbon leading away from the harsh demands of the cliffs.

It was there, amidst the swirl of unfamiliar faces, the scent of cheap perfume and stale beer, and the scratchy strains of a distant band, that he spotted her. Ellie. She stood behind a folding table, serving lemonade, her brown hair tied back simply with a ribbon, a few stray tendrils escaping to frame her face. She had a quiet confidence that made her stand apart, a self-possession that seemed to hold its own against the swagger of most soldiers. Her eyes, a warm, deep brown, held a spark of intelligence and a hint of curiosity.

Most soldiers didn't impress her; their bravado often fell

flat. But Johnnie was different. He was quiet and observant, his gaze steady and intelligent, a calm presence in the bustling hall.

When he approached her table and, with hesitant politeness, asked her for a dance, she looked at him, almost as if she were looking inside him, and said, "No."

Johnnie's heart dropped.

"I'll go for a walk though," Ellie offered, "it's so hot and noisy in here - I get off in 10 minutes."

Johnnie waited, and soon, they were walking together on a warm, star-lit night.

"It's so different here," Johnnie admitted, his voice a little softer than he intended. "Not much like where I grew up."

Ellie smiled faintly. "Oh? And where's that?"

"Up in the Adirondacks," he told her, his gaze drifting to the vast, dark sky above. "Mountains mostly. Snow, pure and cold. We'd climb them, ski down. It's a strange kind of beauty, I suppose. Not many folks understand it."

"I think I might," Ellie replied, her voice gentle. "Our farm, it's not mountains, but it's close to the land. You learn its rhythms, the seasons. The smell of fresh hay, the rustle of corn stalks in late summer, the earthy scent of potatoes being dug from the soil, and the sweet, sharp aroma of apples ripening in the orchard. The quiet dignity of work. It gets into your bones, doesn't it?"

Johnnie nodded, a profound sense of understanding settling between them. They spoke of futures that felt both distant and intimately real, intertwined by shared silences and nascent understanding.

As they walked, Johnnie noticed the unusual "X" shaped necklace she wore. "That's a unique necklace," he pointed to it. "I've never seen one quite like it."

Ellie touched it, her fingers tracing the shape. "It's a St. Andrew's Cross," she explained. "My older brother, he's in the Navy, gave it to me when I graduated high school. It's special.

The X shape, resembling the Roman numeral 10, originates from St. Andrew and reflects our family's Scottish heritage. It's even on the Scottish Flag."

She paused, a thoughtful look on her face. "It's a coincidence, actually. It looks a bit like the crossed bayonets emblem of your 10th Mountain Division patch, doesn't it?"

Johnnie's eyes widened slightly. "It does," he murmured, a feeling of peace washing over him. "I hadn't noticed that."

"I like coincidences," Ellie said softly, her gaze meeting his. “My mother always says they happen when God is smiling at us —a little wink to remind us to have faith."

Johnnie was deeply touched.

His hand lightly brushed hers, and she softly took his hand.

They walked hand in hand together for the first time, the quiet companionship a balm to his soul, a stark contrast to the relentless demands of his training.

32

HOLDING ON

It was late summer at Seneca Rocks when Johnnie saw the familiar faces-Mineo and Luby-arriving for their turn at the rocks. Their expressions reflected the same eagerness and apprehension Johnnie remembered from his first days.

Tech Sergeant McCaffrey pushed them through the rigorous 14-day program, starting on the sturdy wooden "corn cribs" before progressing to the imposing quartzite blade itself. He taught them knot-tying by lantern glow, precise anchor placements, and the quiet, deliberate strikes of pitons. He made them climb silently, like shadows.

On their last Friday night, after their final brutal day of rappelling and handhold work, the chill of evening settling in, they huddled with Johnnie around a crackling fire.

The flames licked at the darkness, casting long, flickering shadows across the surrounding rocks. The scent of the firewood mingled with the metallic tang of sweat—a comfort against the night's cool mountain air.

Mineo winced as he flexed his bruised and swollen knuckle. "I swear this rock has it out for me," he muttered, holding his hand up to the fire.

Luby, who had been staring quietly into the flames, suddenly spoke, his voice uncharacteristically low. "My kid brother, Bill. He was scared of the dark. Cried when the lights went out."

He poked the fire with a stick, sending a shower of sparks into the air. "One night, the power went out in a storm. Bill was in the bunk bed above mine, hysterical. So, I started telling him the dumbest jokes I could think of. 'What did the farmer say when he saw three holes in the ground? Well. Well. Well.' Stuff like that. Stupid, right? But he started laughing. And as long as he was laughing, he wasn't crying. Finally, he fell asleep. I guess I just figured... as long as I could keep him laughing, I could keep him from thinking about the dark."

He looked up, and for a fleeting second, the familiar glint in his eye was gone, replaced by something older and sadder. "Bill's on a ship out in the Pacific now." He blinked, and the moment was gone. The light-hearted smile returned as he pulled a can from his pack.

"Anyway. Who's hungry? I've got the Army's finest delicacy right here: Shoulder of Pork and Ham." He balanced a small pan on the flames. "Dinner is served."

Mineo groaned. "How the hell do you eat that stuff? Seriously—what is that?"

Luby shrugged and flipped a slice with the edge of his knife. "It's SPAM," he said, proud. He speared a piece and took a bite. "Think about it—pre-cooked, ready to go, hot or cold. This stuff's a lifesaver in the field."

Johnnie chuckled as he pulled his jacket tighter. As far as he knew, every soldier except Luby hated SPAM—that gelatinous brick of meat. The running joke was that it was so tough it could survive a direct hit from a howitzer.

"Man, Johnnie," Mineo said, turning to him with a shake of his head, ignoring Luby's dinner. "You make this look easy.

We've gotten good, sure, but you... you just float. It's like you belong up there."

"Yeah," Luby added with a mouthful of SPAM, "like a mountain goat. So what's the trick? What's your secret to being a great climber?"

Johnnie smiled slightly. "It's *Holding On*."

Mineo and Luby exchanged a look.

Johnnie leaned back. "Remember I told you about Rolf Monsen back at Lake Placid? He said the secret to being a great skier was *Falling*. Said if you weren't falling, you weren't learning. You weren't pushing the edge. You were playing it safe. But to really grow, to be *great*, you had to reach past the limits—even if it meant falling flat."

He picked up a small stone and tossed it into the fire, watching sparks crackle into the night.

"Here at the rocks, it's not about falling. It's about *holding on*. But the idea is the same. You hold on for as long as you can until you feel your grip about to go. You push until your strength runs out. That's when you learn something real—about the rock, and yourself."

Johnnie stared at the fire for a while, going someplace from his past, then said, "It becomes instinct, like a squirrel leaping limb to limb. He doesn't *think* about the next jump—he *knows*—he just instinctively knows he can make that next leap. That's what we're after. That limit-testing. That knowing."

Mineo glanced over. "Speaking of limits—what's with Tech Sergeant McCaffrey dragging you instructor guys out of bed in the middle of the night?"

Johnnie gave a wry smile. "He likes surprises. Wakes us up at midnight, no moon, no light—just gear up and climb. One of the hardest faces. No noise, no talking. Just feel your way up. Then at the top, we practice with those new A4 sniper rifles with the Weaver scopes."

He dropped into a low, gravelly impression: "Alright, Grey.

Two hundred yards. There's your target. In the damn dark. Miss and you're climbing this rock again before sunrise."

Mineo snorted. "McCaffrey always says, 'If you can't make it to the top, then you can't take the shot. Or something like that.' It makes sense. You're one of the few who can make it."

Luby looked at Johnnie thoughtfully. "You do any hunting growing up?" Johnnie's expression dimmed. "Yeah... a bit," he said, adding nothing more, and stared far away into the fire.

Luby paused, chewing slowly, his eyes distant as if something had just occurred to him. Mineo and Johnnie waited, expecting a joke or some offhand remark. Luby then glanced at Johnnie for a moment as though he was just about to ask something, then thought better of it and let it go. "C'mon," Mineo nudged. "Out with it."

Luby blinked, then grinned, choosing the easier path. "Nope, I'm eating."

He timed it perfectly. They laughed and gently threw their empty cups at him.

33

MILK BOTTLES

The weeks passed, each one punctuated by Johnnie's visit to Ellie's family's farm. He visited her every chance he could, drawn by a pull as strong as any mountain current, a yearning for the quiet comfort he found with her.

Sometimes, he'd show up dusty and tired from training, boots worn from miles of climbing, his uniform smelling of sweat, a clear departure from the clean, rural air of the farm.

Ellie would often be in the pasture, her hands capable and strong as she tended to the dairy cows, collected eggs from the chickens, or helped her father pick and press apples into cider. Alternatively, she might be in the warm, bustling kitchen, where the scent of baking bread offered a welcoming embrace, often accompanied by the aroma of chicken and beans simmering with spices from the garden.

One afternoon, he found her in the barn, her brow furrowed as she struggled with a stubborn cow.

"Need a hand with that, Miss Ellie?" Johnnie offered, a smile playing on his lips.

Ellie looked up, a lock of hair falling across her face. "Oh,

Johnnie! You startled me. And yes, please. This one's being particularly difficult today." She gestured to the cow. "Ever milked a cow before?"

Johnnie chuckled, shaking his head. "Can't say I have. Squirrels, yes. Cows, no."

Ellie laughed, a clear, joyful sound. "Well, there's a first time for everything." She guided his hands, warm and soft, over the udder. "Like this. A gentle squeeze, a rhythm."

Johnnie fumbled, startled as the warm, pulsing flank brushed against him, nearly losing his balance. Ellie laughed again, wiping foam off his boots with a gentle hand.

Before he could recover, she leaned in and kissed him, the taste of hay and sweetness on her lips. It was a simple moment, but it cemented something profound between them.

They walked along wooded trails, their hands brushing against each other. The quiet companionship was a comfort to his soul, a welcome relief from the relentless demands of his training. They watched fireflies blink in the dusk, tiny, fleeting lights against the encroaching darkness.

"Do you ever think about what comes after all this?" Johnnie asked one evening, his voice low, as they sat on the porch swing. "The war, I mean. What then?"

Ellie leaned her head on his shoulder. "Sometimes. I imagine a quiet life. Here, maybe. Or somewhere new, if that's where you need to be. As long as we're together."

"That sounds... good," Johnnie murmured, a warmth spreading. "Really good."

Her family liked him, their quiet approval a comfort, a sign that he was genuinely welcome.

Her dog, "Bear," a wary old hound, didn't bark at him, a clear sign of acceptance, a trust earned. It felt right—like coming home, a feeling he hadn't fully realized he was missing.

34

TRUST FALLS AND TEAMWORK

As the training at Seneca Rocks escalated, so did the danger, a constant, sharp edge to their days. The instructors kept training, too. Advanced exercises featured tension cable crossings, suspended precariously between cliff edges and swaying high above the canyon floor, presenting a dizzying test of courage and balance.

Medical evacuation drills became frighteningly realistic, teaching them to stabilize a broken leg with a coil of rope, to lower a stretcher off a dizzying ledge, to move as one unit up the face of Seneca in total silence, a single, living organism, each man relying on the next with absolute faith.

One day, the lead instructor, a hardened veteran with eyes that had seen too much, slipped deliberately mid-climb, his carefully orchestrated fall sending a jolt of panic through the team.

They caught him instantly, their belay lines snapping taut, their muscles screaming, their trust absolute, a testament to countless hours of practice.

"You trust each other or you die," he said, brushing dust from his uniform.

His voice was calm, the lesson stark and undeniable, etched into their minds. "Simple as that."

The words resonated with a chilling truth, a truth they were learning with every climb, every shared risk.

35

A WEEKEND ROUTINE

As the weeks at Seneca Rocks turned into months, Johnnie fell into a comforting routine, a rhythm of life. His weekends became a pilgrimage to Ellie's farm, a place of hard work, quiet solace, and burgeoning affection.

To bridge the distance, he and Ellie's younger brother, Robbie, a bright-eyed boy with a thirst for knowledge, set about getting Ellie's older brother James's bicycle working again.

"Think we can get this old contraption moving, Johnnie?" Robbie asked, his face smudged with grease as he looked at the rusty bicycle.

Johnnie knelt beside him, examining the flat tire. "We can certainly try, Robbie. Looks like a simple patch job. Got any patch and rubber cement?"

Together, they meticulously fixed the tire and oiled the chain until the gears spun smoothly.

Ellie, watching secretly from the kitchen window, felt a tender warmth spread through her heart; Johnnie was teaching Robbie just as James, away at sea in the Navy, would have done —a subtle, touching echo of family.

Her parents, recognizing the genuine connection and Johnnie's helpfulness, readily allowed him to use James's bike to get back and forth from the base.

Saturdays were spent helping Ellie's father on the farm. Whether it was turning the hay in the fields, digging potatoes from the rich soil, or tending to the rows of beans, cabbage and onions in the vegetable garden, Johnnie found a familiar rhythm in the work.

"You've got a good hand for this, Johnnie," Ellie's father remarked one afternoon, watching him plant corn with practiced ease. "Like you were born to it."

Johnnie grinned, wiping sweat from his brow. "Spent my youth in the Adirondacks, sir. Different kind of work, maybe, but hard work's hard work."

After a day of honest toil, he was increasingly invited to stay the night, sleeping in James's room, a quiet testament to his growing acceptance into the family. Before bed, after Ellie's parents had gone to bed early, Johnnie and Ellie would sneak away to the porch.

There, under the vast, star-dusted sky, they would sit after a fine, home-cooked meal, often sipping sweet cider pressed from the farm's apples, watching the fireflies blink in the dusk.

"Tell me about the mountains again," Ellie often said, her voice soft. "The ones you climb. Do they feel different at night?"

"They do," Johnnie would reply, his voice low. "More mysterious. Like they're holding secrets. But also peaceful, in their own way."

Sometimes, Ellie would read aloud from a book, her voice a soft melody in the night, or they would simply listen to the crackle of the radio, its distant tunes a soundtrack to their quiet intimacy.

They never ran out of things to do or words to share, and both knew, with a poignant ache, that time was slipping by far too quickly.

36

CRUTCHES

Each trainee climbing class lasted two intensive weeks. The first week was entirely dedicated to foundational rope techniques and training on the wooden towers constructed during the camp's establishment.

It was a brutal weeding-out process: at the end of week one, each instructor was tasked with cutting four of their ten trainees, who would then be sent back to Camp Hale, their expert rock climbing dreams deferred.

At the start of one week, with the Appalachian summer still heavy in the air, Johnnie, now a seasoned instructor, found himself atop a wooden climbing tower, one of the "corn cribs" the farm boys had so aptly named. He guided his team through the intricate dance of rope work and belaying, his voice calm and authoritative as he demonstrated techniques.

As Johnnie watched his team, his gaze drifted across the training grounds. In the distance, he was surprised to see Hogan, his friend from Camp Hale, attempting to climb another corn crib. Johnnie turned back to training his team and thought of their days back in Colorado.

Then, Johnnie turned back to glance at Hogan. He had a

premonition, and then, almost in slow motion, Hogan's handhold failed. A sickening crack echoed across the training field, followed by sounds of horror from nearby men as Hogan fell to the ground, his leg snapping beneath him.

Without a moment's hesitation, Johnnie rappelled down his corn crib faster than anyone had seen, hitting the ground and sprinting towards his friend.

They quickly got Hogan to the medical tent, where his leg was put in a large, heavy cast and reset. The grim reality of the injury meant Hogan was given orders back to New Jersey, to an R&R facility near his hometown of Bloomfield.

A couple of days later, on Friday, after classes ended, Johnnie went to visit him before he was sent home. Hogan told him how upset he was about washing out. Then he says, "You know, since I'm no longer a student, maybe you can take me into town tonight?" Hogan always had a bit of a thirst for trouble, and he played the sympathy card on Johnnie perfectly.

Johnnie had meant to commiserate with Hogan about washing out, but the moment they hopped into the bar he was immediately taken aback. It was as if a switch had flipped: Hogan's face, only moments before etched with disappointment, now lit up with unbridled joy. Within minutes—despite his cumbersome cast and crutches—he'd caught the eye of a beautiful girl and her friend across the crowded bar.

"Hold my beer," Hogan announced, a broad, confident grin spreading across his face. "I see the girl I'm going to marry." With that, he hoisted himself up and, with remarkable agility for a man on crutches, hopped over to the bar.

Johnnie just sat there, bemused, watching the scene unfold. Hogan returned a few minutes later, beaming. "She's from Montclair, NJ, Johnnie," Hogan beamed, "she's loaded! She's here visiting her brother, who's some big muckie muck civilian contractor for the Army."

Johnnie looked at his friend, so entirely confident and so

full of unrestrained joy, and did not doubt that Hogan was genuinely going to do precisely what he said and marry that girl.

As Hogan hopped back over to see the future, Mrs. Hogan, Johnnie watched them and thought to himself, you could just see the love and spark between them; it was electric and palpable. Any stranger who walked in would notice it.

This moment, electric and undeniable, mirrored the night he'd met Ellie. A profound certainty, warm and unwavering, settled deep in Johnnie's soul: he wanted to spend the rest of his life with Ellie. It wasn't a sudden thought, but the quiet, undeniable echo of a truth his heart had always known, now finally articulated in his mind.

Hogan hopped back over to Johnnie, his triumphant return pulling Johnnie from his reverie. 'Hey, Johnnie,' he said. "How'd Luby and Mineo do when they went through the rocks?"

Johnnie took a sip of his beer, a faint smile playing on his lips. "Technically, they're two of the best who ever came through here...." He stopped, letting the words hang in the air.

Hogan leaned forward, with anticipation. "But?"

"But," Johnnie continued, "they were trained by McCaffrey, who encouraged them to test new things, try out new stuff to find ways to be even quieter."

Johnnie took another, longer sip of beer.

"And?" Hogan prompted, a mischievous glint in his eye.

"They almost got kicked out because Luby used Mineo's underpants to muffle the sound of hammering in the pitons."

"He did not!" Hogan exclaimed as he snorted a laugh and almost spat out his beer.

Johnnie grinned, shaking his head. "Oh, he did."

Johnnie continues. "Then Mineo got a hold of some beets, and dyed all of Luby's underwear pink."

He takes a sip of beer, then continues. "So, McCaffrey calls Luby and Mineo, has them standing at attention in front of the whole squad, and chews them out—up, down, and sideways. And, you know what Luby says to McCaffrey?

He says, "Sarge, you told us to try new things."

Hogan's laughter trailed off, replaced by genuine concern for his friend Luby, and he asks: "What did McCaffrey do?"

Johnnie's eyes softened at the thought of a fond memory. "McCaffrey just threw up his hands and walked away ... and he never told students to try new things after that."

"Classic Luby," Hogan chuckled, shaking his head, a broad smile still on his face.

37

THE SMITH FARM

One blustery afternoon, a sudden, torrential rainstorm swept over the Appalachian hills, turning all the dirt roads into treacherous quagmires.

Johnnie, visiting Ellie's farm for the weekend, found himself knee-deep in mud, straining alongside Ellie's father to free the tractor from a giant, sucking hole.

They had been trying to plow a new section for planting corn, but the heavy rains had turned the rich earth into a clinging trap. His uniform was soaked through from the rain.

"Just a little more, Johnnie!" Ellie's father said as he shifted the engine from forward to reverse and back, trying to rock the tractor out of the rut. "Almost got it!"

Johnnie pushed, his muscles screaming. "This mud's got it good, sir!"

Johnnie put all his impressive might into it, and the tractor spun forward out of the deep rut, kicking up a wall of mud all over Johnnie in the process. His uniform, formerly just wet from the rain, was now thoroughly caked in mud.

Back at the farmhouse, Ellie's mother insisted he change.

"Goodness, Johnnie!" Ellie's mother exclaimed, seeing his

state. "You're soaked to the bone! Come in, come in. We can't have you catching your death."

She bustled about, pulling out a pair of James's pants. "These might fit," she said, holding them up. "They're dry and clean. Go on, get out of those wet things."

That evening, with the rain still drumming on the tin roof, Johnnie and Ellie found themselves curled up on blankets on the floor near the crackling warmth of the fireplace, the soft glow illuminating their faces as they talked late into the night.

"It's cozy in here," Ellie murmured, leaning her head on his shoulder. "Much better than being out in that storm." "Couldn't agree more," Johnnie replied, feeling the fire's warmth spread through him.

In the morning, Ellie's mother surprised them, smiling, with Johnnie's uniform. "Johnnie, for you," she said, her voice warm. "All clean and pressed. And thank you, truly, for helping my husband with that tractor yesterday. You were a godsend."

She then gestured for him to follow her into the kitchen, and as he followed, he caught the intoxicating aroma of freshly baked apple pies—two huge golden-crusted beauties, their warmth radiating. "I made a couple of apple pies," she said, "please, take them back to the boys in camp. They'll appreciate a taste of home, I'm sure."

Johnnie's eyes widened at the sight and smell of the pies. "Mrs. Smith, these look incredible," he said, his voice had been filled with genuine awe. "And thank you for my uniform. You're a miracle worker." "Nonsense," she waved her hand. "Just a little something. You boys are doing important work."

Johnnie, with the pies carefully nestled in the front basket of James's bike, pedaled back to camp, the sweet scent of the pies wafting to his nose. He entered the breakfast tent, where the instructor's eyes widened at the sight of Johnnie and his aromatic cargo.

"Who wants pie?" Johnnie announced, a grin spreading across his face.

The instructors, a hardened bunch, all gave Johnnie a tiny, almost imperceptible salute. One gruff voice, perhaps McCaffrey's, muttered, "God Bless You, Johnnie Grey."

The small salute, reminiscent of Mr. Sandford's greetings and farewells, brought a sudden wave of homesickness to Johnnie but also deep happiness at how far he had come.

HIS PERFORMANCE as an instructor hadn't gone unnoticed, and the apple pie didn't hurt. The following week, in May 1944, Tech Sergeant McCaffrey called him into the command tent. "Grey," he said, skipping any preamble. "You've earned these." He slid a set of Staff Sergeant stripes across the table. "You're turning out the best climbers we've got. Keep it up.

38

HOME - PART II

June 1944

The Adirondack air, crisp and familiar, filled Johnnie's lungs as the car pulled up to the small cabin. He had managed to secure a short leave, a precious few days away from the relentless training, and his heart pounded with the anticipation of surprising his mother and Allee.

As he hopped out of the car in his full uniform, he thanked the driver for giving him a lift from the bus depot. And he saw a sight that both warmed and unsettled him: his mother was on the porch, engaged in quiet conversation with Mr. Sandford, the old school bus driver. He hadn't expected anyone to be there, let alone Mr. Sandford.

Things had been changing in Lake Placid, too, he realized, even in its quiet corners.

His mother looked up - her eyes widened, a gasp escaping her lips, and then she was running across the yard, her arms wide. She threw herself into his embrace, hugging him with all her might, her face buried in his uniform, tears streaming down her cheeks.

"Oh, Johnnie! My boy, my boy!" she sobbed, holding him so tight he could barely breathe. "I wish I'd known you were coming! I would have prepared something! And Allee, she just went into town. She's the new schoolteacher, you know, Mrs. Fairchild retired. She's taken to it like a duck to water. The children adore her, and it's a blessing to see her so fulfilled, bringing a little extra into the house too."

After the initial joyous embraces and tearful reunions, a more somber quiet settled. His gaze drawn to Mr. Sandford's prosthetic hand, Johnnie found the courage to ask a question that had weighed on him for years.

"Mr. Sandford," he began, his voice low, "were you with my dad when he got wounded? Would you... tell me the story?" Mr. Sandford looked at Johnnie's mother, a silent question in his eyes. She gave a slight, almost imperceptible nod, her face tightening, and then excused herself, murmuring, "I don't think I can hear it again right now," before disappearing inside.

Mr. Sandford sighed, his gaze distant, lost in the grim landscape of memory. "We were in the trenches, Johnnie. Hand-to-hand. Brutal stuff. We thought we'd made it through; the fighting had died down—and then... it got quiet. Too quiet. That's when the mustard gas came."

He paused, his voice thick with the weight of the past. "There were these thuds and pops—mortar fire. Then a whistling. When the shells hit the ground, it wasn't like smoke. It was this oily cloud—a mix of vapor and liquid that clung to everything, seeping into every crevice. The smell—like mustard, garlic, or horseradish—hid how deadly it was."

He looked away for a moment, swallowing. "Your dad saw me fumbling—couldn't get my mask on. My hand was already mangled. He didn't hesitate. Dropped his own mask to help me with mine. By then the gas was getting thick, and he was breathing it in. We crawled, felt for his mask in the mud, found it, got it on him. But it was too late, Johnnie. His lungs were already burned. He coughed—this terrible, rattling sound—and his skin began to blister."

He exhaled slowly, voice shaking. "He made it home. But the gas had taken hold, deep in his lungs. It got worse after Allee was born—every breath a battle. He came home, but the gas, the wounds... they came with him. He died. Quietly. We didn't talk about it, Johnnie. Some things, you just carry. You don't want to burden the living with that kind of death."

Mr. Sandford's voice cracked. "He saved my life, Johnnie."

Johnnie felt a raw, searing pain erupt in his chest. Tears streamed down his face, silent sobs shaking his frame. Mr. Sandford, too, began to cry, the shared grief a heavy presence between them.

Just then, Johnnie's mother reappeared, her eyes red, and without a word, she joined them, pulling them both into a tight embrace. The three of them stood there, clinging to each other, a silent testament to shared loss and enduring love.

Finally, Mr. Sandford pulled back, his eyes still wet but resolute. "Johnnie," he said, his voice gravelly, "from what I hear, this one's worse. You take care of yourself, son."

39

HOME - PART III

The following day, the sun streamed through the kitchen window, casting warm light on the worn table. Johnnie's mother, her face softer than it had been the night before, looked at him.

"Skip church today, Johnnie," she said gently. "Tell me more about your life since you left Lake Placid."

Johnnie and Allee had caught up the night before, but Allee had left earlier that morning to teach Sunday School at St. Eustace's Episcopal Church.

Johnnie, grateful for the reprieve and the chance to share, began to recount his adventures. He told her about Camp Hale, the biting cold, the thin air, and the antics with Luby, Mineo, and Hogan. He described their personalities, their jokes, and the strange, unexpected camaraderie forged in the crucible of mountain training.

His mother listened, her eyes twinkling with laughter as she recalled their escapades. "Oh, Johnnie," she chuckled, "I feel like I know them already!"

But mostly, he talked about Ellie. He spoke of her quiet strength, her family's farm, and how hard it was for them all without her older brother, James, away in the Navy. He also acknowledged how difficult it must be for her and Allee to have Johnnie away training for war.

His mother laughed, a warm, reassuring sound. "I'm fine, Johnnie. We're fine. All we do is worry about you." Her gaze softened, filled with an immeasurable love.

"I love you, son, more than every breath and heartbeat. Please, go live your life, stay safe, but keep going. What was it that Darby used to say?" She smiled, a shared memory passing between them. Johnnie nodded, a quiet, powerful promise forming on his lips. "See you at the top."

"Edgar Darby is one smart boy," she murmured, and Johnnie wholeheartedly agreed. "You know he visited with Allee last time he was home on leave from West Point."

Johnnie thought Darby was being kind, a friendly visit, and nothing more. The subtle suggestion of his mother's words, of a deeper connection between Darby and Allee, would only settle in his mind much later.

Johnnie got up to hug his mom and kiss her goodbye. As he prepared to hitchhike back to the train station in town, he heard a familiar yet almost forgotten rumble. The old yellow school bus, a relic of his childhood, turned the corner.

He looked at his mother, a puzzled expression on his face. "What's this?" She smiled, a little surprise playing on her lips. The bus hissed to a stop, and Mr. Sandford swung open the door, his eyes twinkling.

"Where to, Johnnie?" he asked. "The train station, Mr. Sandford," Johnnie replied, a wide grin breaking across his face. He stopped, stood tall, and gave Mr. Sandford a crisp, full salute. Mr. Sandford, his face beaming, returned the salute with equal pride.

As the train pulled away, his mother, Mr. Sandford, and Allee running to see him off in her Sunday finest, stood waving, their voices carrying on the wind, "I love you!" Johnnie leaned out the window, his heart full, and called back, "I love you too. See you at the top!"

A FEW WEEKS LATER, a letter from Allee arrived. She told him about June 6, 1944, the day the invasion of Normandy was announced. The church bells, she wrote, had tolled all morning. She included a clipping from the *Lake Placid News* titled **D-Day Prayers.** It described how the whole village had stopped to pray for the boys overseas. Reading her words, Johnnie could picture it perfectly. He was one of those boys they were praying for now.

40

GOODBYE

Back at the Rocks, the orders came without fanfare, a terse slip of paper delivered by a grim-faced Corporal. Italy.

The Front.

The words hung in the air, heavy with meaning, a sudden, sharp shift from theoretical training to the brutal reality of combat. Johnnie packed in silence, his movements efficient and practiced. Each item folded, each strap tightened, a small act of defiance against the surging tide of war.

He went to see Ellie one last time.

The farm was quiet; the only sound was the soft rustle of autumn leaves, a gentle whisper of farewell.

She stood in the barn doorway, arms crossed, shoulders hunched, and her eyes red-rimmed, as if she had known this moment was coming for weeks—a premonition she couldn't escape. "I knew it was coming," she said, barely a whisper, thick with unshed tears.

He nodded, unsure what to say, the usual easy words caught in his throat, choked by the enormity of the moment.

Ellie started to take off the St. Andrew's Cross necklace her brother had given her, and she draped it over Johnnie's head.

He asked, "What are you doing?"

"I want you to have something to remember me by - and to keep you safe."

He protested, "You've already given me so much, I can't take this - this is from your brother."

She smiled, a sad, knowing curve of her lips. "It's like one of those trail marks you told me about. Wherever you get sent, and regardless of whatever happens to you, use it to find your way back to me, Johnnie Grey."

Johnnie's eyes welled up, and when he caught his breath, a raw, heartfelt whisper escaped him. "I love you."

Ellie, with a twinkle in her eye, said, "See you at the top."

His heart dropped for a moment—she did not reply, "I love you." Then she pulled him close and whispered in his ear, "That means I love you more."

He held her close, burying his face in her hair, breathing in her scent—the scent of home, of everything he cherished, the very reason he was heading into the storm.

He turned and walked away, the smell of hay and her quiet strength clinging to him like a phantom warmth, a memory he would carry into the cold, distant war.

41

BOUND FOR NAPLES

December 1944

On 2 December 1944, Staff Sergeant Johnnie Grey and the 86th Regiment arrived at Camp Patrick Henry, the Virginia port of embarkation, stepping into air thick with the damp chill of the Atlantic coast.

The docks presented a chaotic ballet: throngs of soldiers in olive drab, mountains of duffel bags, and the constant, oily thrum of engines.

Their journey to Italy would be aboard the *USS America*. On 11 December, Johnnie, along with the rest of the 86th, filed up the gangplank of the troop transport.

Once aboard, a welcome piece of news rippled through the ranks of the assembled men: their pay would increase by 20% for overseas duty. For instance, a Private First Class would see his monthly pay jump from $54.00 to $64.80.

As he reached the top of the gangplank, a familiar sight met his eyes. Sergeant Mineo leaned against the railing, his face a sickly shade of green, even before the ship had left the dock.

Corporal Luby, ever the loyal companion, struggled with Mineo's bags, muttering under his breath.

"Well, well, if it isn't the happy couple," Johnnie jested, a tired grin spreading across his face. "Looks like you two are already enjoying your cruise."

Mineo sickeningly groaned a weak, pathetic sound. "Don't even start, Johnnie. I swear, the smell of this boat is enough to make a dead man seasick. And good to see you too, sir."

"He's been like this since we saw the waterline," Luby sighed, dropping Mineo's bag with a thud. "I'm starting to think he's just putting it on so I have to carry his gear."

All three shared a brief, genuine laugh, a moment of levity amidst the sobering fact of their deployment.

They found a spot on deck, watching the receding coastline. The conversation quickly turned to their destination. "Northern Italy, huh?" Mineo said, his voice still a bit strained. "Heard the Fifth Army's bogged down. Generals got some big plan to break the stalemate."

Luby nodded, with a serious expression on his face for a moment. "Yeah, rumors are flying. They say it's gonna be a real paradise. But hey," he added, a mischievous glint returning to his eyes, "I'll trade all my beloved cans of SPAM for dinner and a dance with one of those beautiful busty dark-eyed Italian girls Mineo dreams about."

Mineo looked at him and decided whether to say something back but just smiled to himself and said, "Amen to that."

42

A LETTER FROM HOME

On 22 December, after what felt like an eternity of gray waves and the thrum of engines, the *USS America* finally docked in Naples. The harbor assaulted the senses with unfamiliar sights and sounds, offering a chaotic welcome to the Italian theater.

The Naples pier buzzed with activity, and the air hit them with a jarring blend of salt, diesel, and a thousand strange smells—some enticing, like food cooking nearby, while others were foul and unsettling.

Amidst the endless crates and shouting stevedores, the call for 'Mail!'—a word that could make a man forget the war for a precious second—echoed through the crowded bunks.

A Corporal, weary yet methodical, began the slow, sacred ritual of distributing the precious envelopes. Johnnie watched, his anticipation tightening, and then he felt relieved when a few landed near him.

One stood out; the familiar, precise script seemed almost to pulse with a connection to home. His breath caught. Darby. Johnnie tore it open, a rare smile touching his lips. He read.

Dear Johnnie,

I hope this finds you before you're too far along. I wanted to give you a heads-up: my West Point class was cut short. They rushed us through and graduated us early, actually on D-Day, and now we're all commissioned. So when this whole mess is over, and we get back to Lake Placid, I expect plenty of saluting from you. Don't forget your manners now that I'm an officer and all.

The playful jab was pure Darby, and Johnnie chuckled, a sound that felt foreign in the grim setting of the troop transport. However, the tone then shifted to become serious, almost solemn.

On a more serious note, my old friend, I've been doing a lot of reading here. There is a man named Carl von Clausewitz who wrote a seminal book called "On War." One line has stuck with me; it's something I believe you, of all people, need to know. He wrote: "Routine arises from the mechanical activity of the mind, a tendency to follow a track once it is familiar... In war, it becomes a positive danger."

Think about that, Johnnie. All our training, all the drills—they build routine. But out there, where everything is trying to kill you, routine can get you killed. It encourages unthinking behavior and complacency. Don't let yourself get comfortable; don't let your mind go on autopilot, no matter how familiar the track seems. Always be thinking and constantly adapting. I'm telling you this because I want you to come home.

Say hi to Allee for me when you write home. I ran into her for coffee the last time I was back in town. She's grown into a beautiful young woman. You wouldn't believe it.

Johnnie lowered the letter, a faint, almost imperceptible blush rising to his cheeks. "Well, I'll be," he muttered to himself, a slight, knowing grin spreading across his face. "I think Darby has the hots for my sister." He shook his head, feeling a mix of amusement and happiness for Darby and Allee. He looked back at the letter, the final words echoing in his mind, a familiar promise from a different world.

See you at the top,
2LT, Edgar Darby, US Army

43

THE ROAD TO THE APENNINES

Following their disembarkation in Naples, the troops of the 10th Mountain Division commenced their journey northward towards the Apennine Mountains. This leg of the movement primarily involved a combination of sea and rail transport that felt both ancient and jarringly modern.

Elements of the 86th Regiment, for instance, departed Naples on 14 January 1945. They sailed on flat-bottomed Landing Craft Infantry (LCI) ships, hugging the Italian coastline.

It was a strange sight, watching Italy slide by, a land only seen on maps, knowing that somewhere inland, the real fight was waiting. They arrived in Livorno the next afternoon, 15 January. Other components of the 86th Regiment had gotten there a day earlier, utilizing an old Italian freighter, the *Sestriere*.

From Livorno, the troops traded the sea for the land, piling into military trucks for the final leg of their journey to staging areas situated near Pisa. Some of the other units, it was heard, rode in "forty-and-eights"—those old French boxcars, famously named for their capacity to carry forty men or eight horses.

It was a common sight for troop transport during both

World War I and World War II, serving as reminders of how much has changed and how much hasn't. The trucks rumbled along, finally dropping the men at Staging Area No. 3, about three kilometers west of Pisa, where separated companies finally rejoined the main body.

Between 8 and 11 January, after flying to Naples, General Hays traveled onward to Traversa to meet with Lieutenant General Truscott, the newly appointed commander of the Fifth Army.

Truscott's plan, presented with an almost brutal simplicity, was stark: the 10th Mountain Division would capture Mount Belvedere.

When Hays asked, 'Who is going to share the bullets with us when we attack?' Truscott's answer was chillingly blunt: 'No one.' The finality of Truscott's 'No one' weighed heavily on Hays, the immense burden of the division's isolated task now his alone to bear.

By mid-January, the entire 10th Mountain Division—approximately fourteen thousand men—had quietly moved into and settled in the small villages surrounding the ridges of the northern Apennines.

Life in these forward positions, often in small, war-weary Italian villages, became a tense mix of preparation and waiting.

Days were spent cleaning equipment that had endured the sea voyage and truck transport, meticulously studying maps of the challenging terrain ahead, and undergoing last-minute drills on icy ground.

Nights were invariably cold, with men quartered in cramped, commandeered farmhouses or drafty stone barns, the unsettling sounds of distant artillery a constant reminder of what was to come.

Hot meals were a rare luxury; more often, it was K-rations or C-rations consumed in the damp chill, the anticipation of the coming assault a heavy, unspoken presence among the troops.

Many slept with only four blankets, as sleeping bags were a luxury few possessed, and the snow often lay four to five feet deep, adding to the biting cold.

The 86th Regiment was among the first units of the division to reach the front line, where it relieved Task Force 45—an ad hoc defensive command primarily composed of U.S. antiaircraft battalions converted to infantry (along with attached Brazilian, British, Italian partisan, and African-American elements)—in the Mount Belvedere area just north of Bagni di Lucca.

The 85th and 87th Regiments followed, moving into the area by 20 January.

The journey was over. The work was about to begin.

44

OPERATION ENCORE

February 1945

The makeshift operations room was thick with unspoken tension, illuminated by a bare, dangling bulb and the flickering projection of black-and-white footage. Maps, detailed and vast, covered the walls, marking the slow, brutal crawl of the Italian campaign. A distant fire crackled, its warmth lost to the biting wind howling across the Apennines.

Staff Sergeant Grey, a senior NCO who would lead the reconnaissance mission, sat on the edge of a bench, his jaw tight. He felt the collective weariness in the room and the unspoken question in every officer's eyes: How much longer?

Major General George P. Hays, commander of the 10th Mountain Division, stepped forward, his posture conveying a resolute confidence that filled the dim space, a quiet authority that commanded attention. He tapped a pointer against the large, detailed map of northern Italy, his voice cutting through the low hum of anticipation, sharp and clear.

"This is it, gentlemen. Operation Encore. Our objective:

shatter the last defenses of the German Gothic Line," he announced, the words hanging in the air with immense weight. "This line has held us for months, a network of fortified ridges, concrete bunkers, and machine gun nests embedded in frozen hills, costing us dearly in lives and time."

He paused, allowing the significance of the statement to settle, his gaze sweeping across the grim faces.

General Hays continued, outlining the audacious core of the plan for Riva Ridge. "Our window is short. 18 February to 5 March," he stated, emphasizing the tight timeline and the narrow margin for error. "We take Riva Ridge first—under cover of night. No artillery, no prep bombardment. Stealth. Surprise."

This unconventional approach, a profound departure from typical military doctrine where heavy bombardment often precedes assaults, highlighted the complete reliance on the unique capabilities of the 10th Mountain Division, their specialized training now their only weapon.

The "unscalable" nature of the ridge, as perceived by the Germans, was not an obstacle but a strategic opportunity, transforming a perceived insurmountable barrier into the very element of surprise.

General Hays then directly addressed this German perception: "The Germans think it's unscalable. We are going to prove them wrong."

He detailed the specialized equipment required for the assault: "We climb with full packs and weapons. Ropes, pitons, ladders—whatever it takes."

This emphasis on specialized gear underscored the unique demands placed upon the soldiers and the sheer physical and mental toll it would take.

The subsequent objectives were articulated: "If we can hold the ridge, we can sweep Mount Belvedere and the adjacent Mount Gorgolesco, which would ultimately lead to breaching the line and establishing a forward position in the Po Valley.

General Hays turned to a grainy photo pinned beside the map, allowing the officers to visualize the formidable obstacle. It showed Riva Ridge from the east—jagged rock, sheer drop-offs, and snow clinging to ledges like old gauze, a harsh and terrifying image.

He gestured to the map, tracing the vast expanse beyond the mountains, a vision of open plains after endless peaks. "The Po Valley is the industrial and agricultural heartland for the Axis in Italy. Denying them those resources is critical to their collapse here."

He then pointed to Riva Ridge and Mount Belvedere on the map, his pointer tapping the two crucial points.

"These ridges, gentlemen, overlook key routes into the Po Valley, particularly Route 64, one of only two main paths."

His voice grew more intense, resonating with the weight of strategic importance.

"All the high ground belongs to the Germans, granting their artillery an unobstructed view of our positions. We're exposed at the bottom of a glass fishbowl, with them looking down on us from two-thirds of the rim. But by seizing those peaks, we won't just eliminate their observation posts and artillery-control stations—we'll turn their advantage on its head. We'll clear the path for the Fifth Army to advance, free from constant bombardment and enemy eyes."

He paused.

"This breakthrough will not only shatter their defenses here but will tie down their divisions, preventing them from reinforcing other fronts, and ultimately, contribute to the final push towards Germany."

A murmur rippled through the room as General Hays finished, a collective acknowledgment of the plan's audacious nature, a quiet hum of apprehension and grim determination.

Lieutenant Colonel Henry J. Hampton, a man known for his pragmatic approach, cleared his throat. "General Hays," he began, his voice measured, his gaze steady, "what about reinforcements?"

Other officers, though silent, conveyed their unspoken concerns through subtle shifts in posture, reflecting the perceived "impossibility" of the climb without the overwhelming force of preliminary bombardment, a gamble that felt too great.

Johnnie sat on the edge of the bench, his jaw tight, a muscle working in his cheek, as he listened intently. His internal reaction served as a crucial counterpoint to the external discussions, a silent confirmation of the plan's inherent logic for men like him.

Unlike the general apprehension in the room, Johnnie's perspective was shaped by his unique training and deep understanding of mountain warfare. He understood that what was "unscalable" to others was precisely what he and his comrades had trained for, drawing on years of experience from Camp Hale and Seneca Rocks.

General Hays addressed the question of reinforcements with unwavering conviction, his voice firm and steady.

"They'll come fast, Colonel," he asserted, "But for the first forty-eight hours, you're on your own."

He acknowledged the presence of medics and conditional air support "if the weather breaks," a significant caveat, but firmly emphasized the initial self-reliance of the assault force.

“And it will take six days for our engineers from D Company of the 126th to complete the aerial tramway to the top of the ridge for resupply and to evacuate the wounded from the summit.”

General Hays’s blunt statements underscored the immense physical and psychological pressure on the initial assault force

—the wounded might not be evacuated from the top of the ridge for days.

Hays then reiterated the core principle defining the operation—to dismiss lingering doubts while also validating the entire specialized training of the division.

"But make no mistake—this is a climber's war now. Speed and silence win the ridge." This declaration was the thematic core of Operation Encore, redefining the nature of combat for this specific engagement.

It shifted the focus away from brute force and attrition towards precision, specialized skill, and unconventional tactics. It was the direct validation and payoff of the extensive, unique training undergone by Johnnie and his peers, transforming their niche expertise into the decisive factor.

The briefing concluded with practical actions: maps were handed out, and orders were reviewed. Code words and silent coded hand signals exchanged.

Outside, the wind howled across the Apennines, adding a final touch of foreboding and a reminder of the harsh, unforgiving environment they were about to face.

As the officers filed out into the cold night, their footsteps crunching on the gravel, Johnnie caught Lt. Col. Hampton's eye.

"Think we'll take them by surprise?" Johnnie asked, his voice low, almost a whisper, the question hanging in the frigid air.

Lt. Col. Hampton clapped a hand on Johnnie's shoulder, his grip firm and steady. "If anyone can do it, it's us. We've trained for this at the rocks."

Johnnie nodded, gripping the strap of his rifle, the cold metal a familiar comfort.

His thoughts were not on the cold or the fear but on the rock, the ropes, the climb.

The next ascent wasn't just another climb—it was the start of something bigger. Something final.

Operation Encore had begun.

45

RECON

15 February 1945

The night descended upon the Apennines like a shroud of frigid darkness. With no moon and heavy cloud cover, the peaks and valleys were plunged into an inky, suffocating blackness.

Into this profound void melted a team of six soldiers—Staff Sergeant Grey, Sergeant Mineo, Corporal Luby, Corporal Kaminsky, and two others—becoming six ghosts ascending the formidable eastern face of Riva Ridge.

Their objective was clear—but daunting: a reconnaissance mission to assess enemy strength and gather intelligence on the easternmost peak of Riva Ridge, a summit known to the local villagers as Pizzo di Campiano.

The team knew this was a serious, high-stakes climb—one that demanded technical precision and nerves of steel. They relied on the gear they'd trained with at Seneca Rocks: hemp rope harnesses tied directly to their bodies as belay systems, ice axes, and crampons for the brutally steep sections—some angled between 45 and 90 degrees.

In other places, the mountain offered nothing but sheer vertical rock, demanding pitons hammered silently into cracks, carabiners clipped in to guide the rope and create life-saving anchor points.

On these unforgiving faces, Johnnie, taking point, had no choice but to free climb in the dark—every move untested, every hold a gamble. No one had ever been up this route before. Together, they would forge it—one precarious step at a time.

Johnnie laid out the plan to the team. He'd studied the contour maps from the aerial reconnaissance General Hays had ordered just the day before.

The summit of Pizzo di Campiano rose to roughly 3,175 feet above sea level. Under cover of darkness, they would hike into the Dardagna River valley and reach a staging point of about 1,550 feet. From there, they'd undertake a grueling, highly technical 1,600-foot ascent up the face of the ridge.

This route, he noted grimly, was impassable for mules, meaning every ounce of gear would have to be hand-carried by the men themselves.

"Every 400 feet," Johnnie explained, "we'll tape and tie two knots into the rope we anchor to the rock wall—trail marks to help our 140 climbers track their progress in the dark. During the assault, our Recon team will be positioned along the route to provide guidance: I'll hold position near 1,600 feet at the top. Luby, you're behind me at 1,200; Mineo at 800; Kaminsky at 400. One knot will be tied before each major junction or pitfall. The men are trained to follow the lead climber, but these knots will give them a tactile warning—something they can feel in the darkness—to prepare for what's ahead."

For Johnnie, leading the small elite recon team up at Riva Ridge and placing the guides for others to follow represented a direct application of the discipline forged on the slopes of Whiteface and at Seneca Rocks—lessons from the past now guiding his hands with instinctive precision and directly contributing to the survival of the 140 men who would soon follow.

His gloved hands, calloused and strong, found purchase on the frigid rock face with an almost preternatural intuition, discerning subtle fissures, and barely perceptible holds in the darkness.

Behind him, Mineo and Luby, despite the added burden of their specialized equipment, mirrored his silent efficiency.

Johnnie marked the spots for the pitons, and as they ascended, he meticulously taped and tied knots into the ropes at the designated 400-foot intervals, securing them to the rock wall as vital trail marks.

Johnnie, Mineo, and Luby silently hammered the pitons into the rock with leather-wrapped hammers and soft mallets, just as they'd been trained, to muffle the sound. The three others carried the gear and passed it up the line. With every breath, they repeated McCaffrey's mantra in their minds: 'Not a clink. Not a whisper. Move like shadows.'

The most arduous part of their burden was the EE-8 field telephone wire. Mineo, Luby, and the others each handled a heavy, cumbersome 25-pound spool, carefully paying out the wire foot by foot in agonizingly slow increments and splicing the spool ends as they ascended. This wasn't merely a communication link; it was a strategic artery.

Once they reached the summit, this fragile thread would connect them directly to base camp, allowing them to report enemy positions in real-time and, crucially, to call in artillery strikes with pinpoint accuracy.

Laying it required a delicate balance of speed and stealth, ensuring the line was secure, untangled, and, above all, undetected. Every snag, every potential sound, was a heart-stopping moment of dread.

Hours blurred, muscles screamed, and lungs burned in the

thin air, but the men pushed on, driven by the grim understanding of their mission's importance.

By the time the first faint hint of pre-dawn light began to glow on the eastern horizon, they were nearing their objective, a painstaking, dangerous dance with the mountain nearing its tense climax.

Peering over the summit with binoculars, Johnnie made a series of silent hand signals to Mineo and Luby indicating German locations, troop strength, and heavy weapons, which they wrote down.

When finished, without delay, they rapidly rappelled down the Ridge and quietly raced back to base before the morning's first light.

46

RETURN TO BASE

The descent from Pizzo di Campiano was faster and less perilous. Back on the ground, as they put more distance between themselves and the Ridge, the immediate threat of discovery receded, and the men finally felt the liberating urge to speak.

The biting wind still whipped around them, but now their voices, though hoarse, could cut through it.

"Alright, what's the tally?" Johnnie demanded, his voice rough from the cold, but it was an explicit command. He pulled his scarf down, allowing a plume of frosty breath to escape. "Strength?"

Mineo, ever the meticulous one, shivered but quickly pulled out a small, mud-stained notebook. "Estimated total 40 to 50 German troops, spread out along the 3.5-mile length of the Ridge. German 232nd Infantry Division, and the 1044th Grenadier Regiment. They're dug in deep."

Luby pulled out his notebook and reported, "Lone sentry about 90 yards out. Supporting weapons crews are abundant. At least six machine gun nests 3-400 yards back, mostly MG42s, strategically placed to cover key approaches. Mortars, likely

81mm, were reported to have fired from approximately four positions. And there are forward artillery observers. They're well-concealed, but we've marked their locations where they can be seen."

A grunt of acknowledgment passed through the group. The job was done, the intelligence gathered. The weight of their mission, though physically exhausting, had been successfully carried.

As they trudged on, the snow crunching under their boots, Corporal Kaminsky spoke up, his voice tinged with genuine curiosity. "Hey Sarge, something I've been wondering. Who named this the Gothic Line? The Italians or the Germans?"

Mineo replied, "Oh, definitely the Germans - it's an homage to their ancestors the Goths, an ancient, half-mythical Germanic warrior tribe - calling it the Gothic Line is supposed to make it sound strong, fierce, like it was carved out of the same iron as the Germanic tribes that sacked Rome, shattered legions and brought the Roman empire to its knees. Like it's been here forever, impassable."

No one spoke for a while; they just walked back to base in silence. Then Johnnie said, "We will cross it."

There was a long silence, and they walked on. Then Luby mused softly, "What goes up must come down." They all laughed, not even sure why. Luby just had a knack for expressing things that resonated on multiple levels.

47

THE GERMAN BASE

Feldwebel Kurt Jaeger (E-6) had grown bored of the war, and months of holding this high, fortified position had instilled a dangerous complacency. Their perch on Riva Ridge seemed invincible, a cold, impregnable fortress against the endless Allied push.

He and Gefreiter Emil Hoffman (E-3), his junior, spent their days in a monotonous rhythm of boredom: playing cards, the worn deck a familiar comfort, cleaning rifles with practiced, monotonous movements, and staring out at the endless, indifferent clouds that drifted across the peaks, waiting for nothing to happen.

"You know what I miss, Kurt?" Hoffman muttered, his voice flat, his eyes distant, fixed on some imagined memory. "A warm room. A proper coffee. A hot shower."

Jaeger snorted, a cynical sound that spoke of too many cold nights and too little comfort. "You should be grateful we're up here. We're on top of the world. Would you rather be the poor souls below? Every time they try and climb Belvedere, our spotters call in the heavy guns, and they get swept off the mountaintop like fleas off a dog."

Hoffman chuckled, a hollow sound. "A dog with fleas, you say? Have you ever even had a dog with fleas, Kurt? There's nothing you can do to shake them off."

Jaeger merely harrumphed, exasperated at yet another failed teachable moment with his junior.

48

NIGHT CLIMB

18 February 1945

As the 86th prepared for their night climb up Riva Ridge, Johnnie knew that the men of the 85th and 87th—assigned to the main assault on Mount Belvedere—were facing an order from General Hays that demanded almost unimaginable stealth and brutal, close-quarters resolve.

For the attack on Belvedere, the General's directive was stark: the 85th and 87th would move into position under cover of darkness beginning the night of 19 February. From then until the first light on the 20th, there was to be "no small arms fire... only hand grenades and bayonets." Surprise was everything.

General Hays was willing to shed the blood of the 85th and 87th for a chance at breaking through. He understood the cost —but he believed it was the only way. For the opening assault, he bet everything on silence.

Specially trained for the task, the men of the 85th and 87th were ordered to creep up the mountain under cover of darkness, getting close enough to strike. But once in position, they were to wait—holding silently for hours in the freezing dark.

Just before dawn, they were to charge from close range, using bayonets and hand grenades to overwhelm the enemy before the Germans even knew they were there.

It was a brutal gamble. But the Fifth Army had already tried the safer path—rifles, mortars, artillery, long-range bombardment—and none of it had dislodged the Germans from Field Marshal Kesselring's heavily fortified perch.

Tonight, though, it was the 86th's turn. They would go first. At approximately 1900 hours (7:00 p.m.), under a deep, moonless sky, Staff Sergeant Johnnie Grey and the original recon team led one of five companies of the 86th—140 mountain soldiers in all—as they hiked silently toward the base of Pizzo di Campiano, deep in the Dardagna River valley.

At the same time, four other companies made the same approach along parallel routes. In total, 700 men would make the climb.

At the base, the strong wind whispered over the Apennines like a living thing, a cold, sharp breath that seemed to carry the very essence of danger as the men tightened their ropes and checked their crampons one last time.

Only the black, featureless silhouette of Riva Ridge loomed ahead, jagged and rising like the immense spine of a sleeping beast—a silent, formidable challenge.

This Ridge, topping out at 4,900 feet above sea level for some of its ascent routes, was famously deemed "unclimbable" by the Germans.

However, the 10th Mountain Division had trained at Seneca Rocks, mastering the discipline of silence under Tech Sergeant McCaffrey, and learning to move like camouflaged ghosts.

By 2200 hours (10:00 p.m.), they had reached the elevated valley floor base where they would begin the 1600-foot ascent to the summit. This steep, icy slope promised to test every ounce of their training.

Using the pre-installed ropes and anchor points, the men ascended in near-total silence.

Lt. Col. Hampton had ordered them, "No talking. No coughing. Pitons are inserted softly and muffled with cloth or leather. The first sound you hear in the next 24-hours better be the sound of victory."

The first soldiers from the 86th began to climb Riva Ridge's limestone and shale, which created an unpredictable and often unstable surface, further complicated by the presence of ice and snow.

Fingers, cold and numb, gripped barely perceptible handholds, seeking purchase in the unforgiving stone. Boots found toe holds the size of coins, their treads seeking purchase on the slick rock, with each movement agonizingly slow and deliberate.

They moved, one section at a time, roped in teams, a single, deliberate organism inching upward, a human centipede against the vertical world. Johnnie reached a narrow ledge, his breath frozen on his scarf, a white plume in the invisible air, his muscles screaming with the effort.

Behind him, a man slipped, a sudden, terrifying scrape of the boot against stone—caught just in time by the taut belay rope, a silent testament to their trust, a life saved by a hair's breadth.

They kept climbing, their ascent measured, inexorable, each footfall a step closer to the enemy.

49

THE FIRST SHOT

Between 0400 and 0500 hours on 19 February, Johnnie and the first wave of his company reached the summit.

Peering over the lip of the ridge, the strong, frigid wind rushed at him and bit at his eyes like razors, tiny, stinging shards of ice. The climb had been silent, brutal, and impossibly steep—the cloak of night had masked their ascent.

Now, with the first faint whisper of morning light catching the eastern sky, he found himself alone belly-flat on top of the ridge. He could feel the cold through his white camouflage uniform, right down to his bones.

But that wasn't what concerned him—he had been trained to ignore the pain from ice and cold.

The ridgeline stretched before him like the spine of some ancient, sleeping beast, still shrouded in the lingering darkness, its contours slowly becoming visible in the emerging light.

Below, nestled in a dugout cleft in the snow, was the enemy. A forward lookout sentry far from the rest of the dug-in Germans atop the mountain—looked utterly unaware.

The man was tired; he shifted his weight, his hands gripped his rifle loosely, a picture of complacency, of a false sense of security. He had no idea Americans had scaled the impossible.

Johnnie reached for the M1903 A4 sniper rifle slung across his back. This was the Army's primary sniper rifle, a bolt-action workhorse, and this one had been fitted with the Weaver Model 330 scope, a 2.5x fixed magnification optic.

He knew its quirks; scopes like the Weaver could sometimes lose their zero under the stress of combat, but a skilled marksman learned to compensate. It had been zeroed for him two days earlier.

He'd spent hours memorizing its response at various ranges, learning how to adjust for wind, for angle, for the steady beat of his breath. Lacking iron sights as the A4 model did to accommodate the scope, proficiency with the optic was paramount. It was a partner, an extension of his will.

He steadied it on a natural rest, a flat rock touched with frost, and slowly rotated the turret on the scope; the clicks were barely audible in the vast silence. He knew the range: 90 yards.

For a Staff Sergeant of his training, hitting a man-sized target at this distance, even under the immense pressure of combat, was quite manageable. The .30-06 Springfield cartridge it fired had a relatively flat trajectory, making a 90-yard shot comfortably within its effective range.

There was a slight decline and a strong wind blowing straight at him—a good thing. It would distort the sound of the shot and carry it back towards him and away from the Germans dug in further away.

He exhaled through his nose to keep the glass clear, his focus narrowing—not just on the target, but on what it would unlock. The shot wasn't the mission. It was a key.

Tech Sergeant McCaffrey's gravelly words from the first day of training echoed in his skull, clear as a bell, a mantra of his training: "I hear you can ski Grey. But, if you can't climb - you can't take the shot."

Johnnie waited.

The German lifted binoculars to his eyes and scanned south toward the valley where Allied artillery screamed. His rifle remained slung on his back. Complacent. Alone. A perfect, unsuspecting target.

Johnnie shifted slightly, minutely adjusting his body to reduce pressure on his elbow—a tiny movement on the grand scale of the mountain but crucial for precision. The cold, strangely, had dulled his nerves just enough to steady him, to bring his focus to a razor-sharp point.

He aligned the reticle—center mass, just beneath the ribcage to account for the upward trajectory, a perfect, deadly cross. He inhaled and held, his lungs burning, the world narrowing to the target and the crosshairs.

Then, with the gentlest pressure—so slow it felt like a thought, a silent command to the rifle—he squeezed the trigger.

The rifle barked like a cracking tree trunk, a shockingly loud sound in the sudden quiet, shattering the dawn. Recoil pushed firmly into his shoulder, a familiar jolt. Through the scope, he saw the German lurch back and fall into the snow like a puppet with its strings severed. There was no flailing, no scream, just the dull thud of finality.

That single, muffled shot was the signal. The 10th was on the ridge. With their surprise assault now underway, the process of blinding the mountain had begun. Neutralizing the German observers here was the key to giving the men on Belvedere a fighting chance.

A second later, silence descended again, profound and absolute, as if the mountain itself held its breath.

No alarm sounded, and no other figures emerged from the unseen bunkers. The Germans had posted a lone sentry at the closest top of the Ridge, confident in the cliffs' protection and blind to the unscalable walls.

But the mountain had betrayed them.

Johnnie's breath came back in sharp, icy gasps—each one a reclaiming of his body.

He glanced down the line at his company of 140 soldiers, still cloaked in shadow, still waiting, their faces etched with grim anticipation. He gave the hand signal.

An infantry whistle pierced the silence, and the message rippled down the line to the five companies of the 86th—each one poised to strike a different summit along the 3.5-mile stretch of the ridge.

The men began to rise like ghosts from the rock, rifles ready, boots quiet against the snow, their movements swift and silent.

As he passed, Johnnie looked down at the fallen sentry—his young face pale in the growing light, as if the life had drained out of him completely.

There was no victory in making the shot. But it had bought his men ninety yards—ninety yards closer to the Germans dug in at the summit.

50

THE SILENT SURGE

19 February 1945

Johnnie and his men rapidly began their run toward the German fortified positions on the Ridge, their boots crunching softly on the fresh snow, each step a muffled whisper. The plan had worked. Surprise, absolute and devastating, was theirs.

The air was still, holding its breath, waiting for the inevitable explosion. They fanned out silently around the perimeter, their movements coordinated and practiced.

A German soldier emerged from a tent, stretching and lighting a cigarette, his eyes unfocused as he searched for what might have caused the subtle faraway sound, distorted and carried away by the breeze, a vague unease stirring within him. He saw Johnnie.

His eyes widened, betraying a flicker of raw terror and dawning comprehension. The man fumbled for his weapon, his hands suddenly clumsy, his mind still grappling with the impossible. Another sniper from the 86th fired a shot that cracked through the morning air, sharp and final. The German collapsed, his cigarette still burning a tiny ember in the snow, a fleeting point of light extinguished.

Johnnie knew the nature of the fight was about to change drastically. He placed his A4 in a sheltered crevice, intending to retrieve it later if possible.

He then unslung his M1 Garand, the standard-issue semi-automatic rifle of the U.S. infantry. This was the weapon for the upcoming fight.

He checked the 8-round en-bloc clip, feeling the reassuring weight of the .30-06 rounds. He knew that with practice, a soldier as adept as he could lay down fire at a rate of 25 to 50 rounds a minute, the rifle firing one round with each pull of the trigger.

He anticipated the distinctive "ping" of the ejected clip after the eighth round. This sound would serve as both a signal to reload and a small, sharp note amidst the growing cacophony of the battlefield.

As the shouts of his men and the answering German fire intensified, Johnnie quickly reached for the M1905 Bayonet sheathed at his hip. The 16-inch blade was a veritable sword. With practiced movements, the cold steel of the bayonet clicking firmly into place on the M1 Garand's lug, his rifle transformed. Now, it was also a spear, ready for the brutal, intimate work of hand-to-hand combat that awaited them in the German positions.

He also instinctively checked his M1911 sidearm pistol, a crucial backup for the desperate moments he knew were coming.

Then chaos.

A sudden, deafening roar broke the silence. Johnnie pushed forward, his M1 Garand now leading the way, a primal surge of adrenaline coursing through him as his training took over.

He remembered Rolf's steady voice on snowy trails, the

broken skis, and the impossible belief he had once placed in a scrawny boy with a slingshot.

With that fire, a cold, burning resolve, Johnnie pressed forward, rallying his men, his voice raw, torn from his lungs. "GO! Charge! Charge!"

Grenades exploded, shaking the ground and sending geysers of snow and rock into the air, transforming the pristine white into a churning, dark mess.

Mortar rounds shrieked through the air like banshees, their descent a terrifying whistle. Machine guns opened up from nests further down the Ridge, their chattering a furious, desperate chorus, a last, defiant stand.

But more Americans were climbing over the top now—hundreds of them, a wave, a relentless tide of white outfitted American soldiers against the white snow, pouring over the lip of the Ridge like an unstoppable force.

The battle was fierce, a close-quarters brawl of desperate men, a maelstrom of shouts and gunshots, like a trapped beast lashing out in its death throes. Germans threw everything they had—shells, flares that burst into eerie, fleeting light, and raw, guttural fury.

But the 10th fought with a different kind of fire, a cold, precise determination forged in the crucible of their training. They cleared the Ridge methodically, seized the high ground, and took prisoners, their faces grimed with powder and sweat, their eyes reflecting the brutal reality of the fight.

The Germans were dazed, stunned to see Americans appear from a slope they'd thought impossible, their eyes wide with disbelief, their minds struggling to comprehend.

By midday on 19 February, Johnnie's company had helped secure its initial objectives on the ridge crest, killing or capturing dozens of Germans, and began digging in. While their surprise assault had been a stunning success, ferocious

German counterattacks immediately jeopardized the division's hold across sections of Riva Ridge.

Intense fighting persisted, but the 86th held its ground. Radio teams, utilizing the telephone lines meticulously placed by the Recon teams on February 15th, immediately began directing artillery fire onto German fallback lines, including targets on Mount Belvedere.

Their newly elevated position on Riva Ridge significantly weakened German spotters' ability to call accurate fire onto the U.S. assault moving up Belvedere.

For their brothers in the 85th and 87th - the 86th had done its job.

For now.

51

THE RIDGE VS. THE MOUNTAIN

As the 10th consolidated its hard-won position on Riva Ridge, the strategic landscape of the Apennines became evident. The two dominant features, Riva Ridge and Mount Belvedere, though geographically close, presented vastly different challenges, each demanding a unique approach to combat.

Riva Ridge, which Johnnie and 700 men had just secured, was a long, narrow crest approximately 3.5 miles in length. Its strength lay in its sheer, "unscalable" eastern face, which the Germans believed offered natural protection, allowing them to rely on scattered outposts and observation points along its length.

It was a defensive barrier, formidable due to its natural incline and the element of surprise that the 10th Mountain Division had so masterfully exploited. The German presence there was primarily for observation and to direct artillery fire onto the valleys below, with their actual dug-in positions being less extensive than what lay ahead.

Mount Belvedere, however, was an entirely different beast. It was not merely a ridge but an entire, hardened base at the summit of a towering mountain. Years of German ingenuity had transformed its peak into a fortress.

Concrete bunkers, interlocking machine gun nests, and hidden minefields were integrated directly into the rock and earth, creating a formidable defensive complex.

Unlike Riva Ridge's outposts, Belvedere represented a deeply entrenched, heavily fortified stronghold designed for prolonged resistance. Its defenses were further amplified by the relentless artillery barrage that created a 'ring of fire'—a continuous, devastating bombardment around its base and slopes, making any direct assault a suicidal endeavor.

To take Belvedere meant not just a climb but a confrontation with a thoroughly prepared and heavily armed enemy in a nearly impenetrable stronghold.

The difference was clear: Riva Ridge was a key to blinding the enemy; Belvedere was the enemy's unyielding heart.

52

BELVEDERE BEGINS

19 February 1945

At 2300 hours, a palpable tension hung in the frigid air of the Apennines. General Hays's audacious plan was in motion: the main assault on the Mount Belvedere complex would proceed without a preliminary artillery bombardment, relying heavily on surprise and the elite skills of his mountain-trained soldiers.

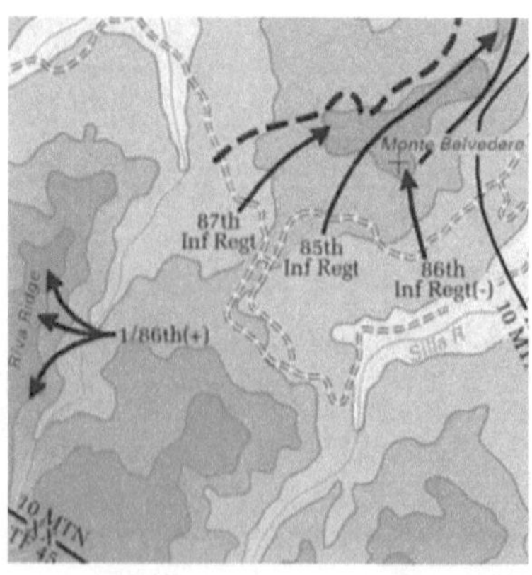

Map: Operation Encore - Initial Phase

The 87th Regiment (approximately 2,700 soldiers) began its stealthy approach under cover of darkness. Its 1st Battalion (around 900 men) faced the daunting task of climbing the sheer western face of Mount Belvedere, aiming for the critical Valpiana Ridge.

Simultaneously, the 2nd Battalion advanced farther northwest toward the villages of Polla and Corona, attempting to outflank the German defenses anchored along the ridgeline. The 3rd Battalion remained in reserve, poised to reinforce the leading elements once a foothold was secured.

Progress was slow, methodical, and grueling—a climb over broken, snow-covered, and often ice-coated rock faces. These were the exact conditions for which they had trained at Camp Hale, often at altitudes exceeding 10,000 feet.

At the same time, to the east of the 87th, the 85th Regiment moved into position. Its 3rd Battalion led the central assault (east of the 87th's 1st Battalion), advancing from the southeast over treacherous terrain toward the summit of Mount Belvedere. Farther east, the 1st Battalion pressed toward Mount Gorgolesco—one of the lynchpins of the German defensive line.

While Riva Ridge had been the first piece of Kesselring's mountain death trap, Mount Belvedere, and Gorgolesco were pieces two and three in Field Marshal Kesselring's interlocking Alpine defense strategy. These were not mere hills but heavily fortified bastions—part of a calculated network of trenches, bunkers, and artillery positions designed to function as an impenetrable death trap.

Under cover of darkness, carrying full 75-pound combat loads, each soldier of the 85th and 87th advanced slowly, carefully, using the three-point climbing technique they had drilled at Camp Hale for steep slopes—always keeping two feet and one hand or two hands and one foot, in contact with the mountain—to avoid falls and to remain undetected. A single misstep could send stones clattering down the slope, betraying their presence.

But still, they climbed—silent, steady, every movement controlled, every breath measured.

Despite the darkness and extreme environmental challenges, they pressed their climb with unwavering vigor. After overcoming initial, scattered pockets of resistance and carefully navigating treacherous minefields, they clawed their way closer to the summits, and then they held in the dark—waiting, silent, just beneath the enemy's positions.

No shots were fired. No lights betrayed them. They had followed orders to the letter.

At first light on 20 February, the men of the 85th and 87th surged from their concealed positions into brutal close-quarters combat—bayonets fixed, grenades hurled with deadly precision.

The 10th Mountain Division had begun its first charge for the stronghold at the summit.

The German defenders, deeply entrenched in a network of mutually supporting machine gun nests, mortar pits often sited in reverse-slope positions for protection, and strategically fortified stone farmhouses converted into miniature fortresses, unleashed a torrent of machine gun and mortar fire.

These reverse-slope emplacements—hidden just behind ridgelines, often dug into gulleys or depressions—were nearly invisible to advancing troops until it was too late. They also allowed the Germans to rain down fire while remaining shielded from observation and return fire.

Tracers stitched the dawn light, and bullets ricocheted off the ancient stone with lethal force.

Though the Germans held the high ground, they were caught completely off guard and driven from key emplacements along the ridgeline. But the price was high—the slopes were littered with the fallen, and the air still throbbed with the violence of the charge.

As the fighting wore on, the tenacity and mountain-honed training of the 85th and 87th began to show. Crucial sections of the ridgeline were now in American hands. The impossible climb had become a foothold—narrow, hard-won, and paid for in blood.

The Gothic line had been cracked. Now the question became: what would the cost be to make it break?

53

THE RING OF FIRE

Despite the hard-won gains on the Belvedere-Gorgolesco ridgeline by the 85th and 87th, the battle rapidly devolved into a brutal, grinding struggle.

The Germans, though initially surprised, reacted with ferocious intensity. The 10th faced severe casualties, not just from the dug-in German defenses but from a relentless, chillingly precise artillery fire originating from batteries positioned safely miles behind their front lines.

These were Field Marshal Kesselring's instruments of attrition: the formidable 4-inch Model 18 cannons, grimly nicknamed 'hammers' by the troops who faced them, and the heavier 6-inch Model 18 cannons, the 'sledgehammers.' These weapons unleashed devastating high-explosive and shrapnel rounds with chilling efficiency.

While the capture of Riva Ridge by Johnnie and the 86th had blinded many German forward observers, the enemy still possessed numerous concealed observation posts and pre-sighted firing solutions. This allowed them to direct their fire with terrifying accuracy, effectively turning any American advance on Belvedere into a lethal gauntlet.

Once an American unit was spotted or even suspected of movement, it became an inevitable target.

The Germans, masters of defensive warfare, had meticulously mapped these approaches. With real-time corrections phoned in or radioed from their remaining observation posts, the first rounds would scream in, landing within 150 meters, the explosions ripping through the air, sending men diving for cover from the hot, jagged shrapnel.

The subsequent rounds, adjusted with deadly precision, would fall within a terrifying 40 meters, often just feet away, leaving virtually no room for escape.

This created what the men began to call the 'ring of fire'—an infernal, seemingly impenetrable corona of destruction encircling Belvedere's hardened bunkers. It was a deadly circular zone, perhaps 400 yards wide, just below the steep summit, churning with ceaseless, indiscriminate destruction.

The air itself became thick and heavy, saturated with the acrid stench of cordite that burned the nostrils and the metallic taste of dust and fear that coated their tongues.

It was a constant, deafening symphony of explosions, the ground shuddering with each impact, a terrifying crescendo of incoming shells that made the earth vibrate incessantly beneath their feet, a deep, guttural thrum that resonated in their very bones and rattled their teeth.

Shells were landing; it felt, every single second, each impact a concussive roar that sent geysers of shrapnel, pulverized rock, and frozen earth into the air, momentarily distorting vision with blinding flashes and swirling, choking debris.

When multiple German guns fired simultaneously, as they often did, their lethal blast and fragmentation zones overlapped significantly within the narrow attack corridors, leaving no haven, no safe inch of ground.

This relentless hail of steel and high explosives formed an almost impassable wall, a curtain of death as inescapable as a tidal wave, trapping American troops in exposed terrain, offering virtually no respite or cover.

The very air thrummed with terrifying anticipation; the constant explosions, the whistling, banshee-like descent of incoming rounds, and the horrifying knowledge that the next blast could be their last made any sustained advance a suicidal endeavor.

The psychological toll was immense, a crushing weight that eroded hope and devoured their very will to fight.

Men who had charged bravely during the initial surprise attacks now hugged the unforgiving earth, looking for cover, their bodies screaming for relief, their minds trapped in a claustrophobic nightmare of noise and concussion.

Every second was a test of nerve, a constant vigilance against an unseen enemy whose deadly precision felt like an inescapable, impersonal judgment.

It was this barrage, more than the mountain's natural defenses, that was grinding the American advance by the 85th and 87th to a near standstill, inflicting hundreds of casualties and shattering morale.

From their precarious perch on Riva Ridge, Johnnie and his men of the 86th could hear and see the terrifying symphony of destruction unfolding across the valley on Belvedere. The night sky above the mountain pulsed with an evil orange glow, the continuous flashes of explosions like heat lightning in a deadly storm.

It was a grim, deafening forecast of their impending ordeal. A cold dread tightened in Johnnie's gut, a familiar knot of fear mixed with grim resignation. He thought of Ellie, her quiet strength, the scent of hay and home, a fleeting image that flickered against the backdrop of the inferno.

The Ring of Fire was not just a barrage; it was, by Field Marshal Kesselring's meticulous design, an inescapable crucible intended to break the spirit, the body, and the life of any who dared to enter.

And the grim reality was undeniable: Johnnie knew, with a cold certainty that settled deep in his bones, that elements of the 86th, his unit, would soon be ordered to advance through the very heart of that deadly ring of fire.

54

BETWEEN TWO MOUNTAINS

20 February 1945

The initial 48-hour onslaught to secure Riva Ridge had finally abated, leaving Johnnie and his men bone-weary but alive. The brutal exhaustion was almost a welcome numbness, a temporary shield against deeper terrors.

As they collapsed amidst the snow-dusted rocks, the "victory" felt hollow, a mere prelude to the inferno unfolding across the valley on Mount Belvedere.

Johnnie watched a line of weary medics attending men, faces he knew, lying on the cold ground, blanket-covered, awaiting the tram to be built in a few days that could take them to the field hospital down below if they could last that long - a stark reminder that even 'taken' ground still claimed its price.

The next battle, it was sickeningly clear, was just beginning across the valley. From their newly won perch, which denied German observers critical vantage points but did not silence all their guns, Johnnie could see the conflagration on Belvedere—a terrifying spectacle of continuous flashes and plumes of oily black smoke against the bruised night sky.

It was a mountain consumed by battle, the distant, percussive rumble of artillery a constant, guttural growl punctuated by the sharper, frantic cracks of machine-gun fire.

Whispers and grim-faced reports from runners painted an awful picture: the brave men of the 85th and 87th Regiments, despite their initial successes in seizing key sections of the ridgeline, were now locked in a desperate struggle, taking severe casualties.

The relentless German howitzers were pulverizing them—the 'hammers' and 'sledgehammers'—and they were crashing against an almost impenetrable wall of Kesselring's concrete bunkers and interlocking machine gun nests.

The mountain, it seemed, was indeed a death climb, chewing through men and hope with equal ferocity. For a moment, Johnnie's mind flashed to the simple blue blazes he'd painted on Whiteface, clear marks on a known path.

Here, the trail was marked only by fire and the screams of the dying, leading into an abyss. What trail mark could guide a man through this?

While other elements of the 86th engaged in vital supporting actions, trying to widen the breach and protect the flanks of the 85th, a cold dread settled in Johnnie's stomach, heavier than any pack he'd carried.

He knew, with chilling certainty, that the call would come for a more direct assault, that his specific unit, or a part of it, would be thrown into that meat grinder.

The thought that he might die on Belvedere wasn't born of cowardice but of a cold, brutal realism honed by the past days of unimaginable combat and the terrifying sights and sounds emanating from the neighboring peak.

He had seen too much and heard too many whispers of the impossible odds. He pulled his worn writing kit from his rucksack, its canvas soft and familiar against his numb fingers—a small piece of home in this desolate landscape.

He found two scraps of dry paper, miraculously unsullied by the battle, tiny, precious rectangles of untouched white. There were things he needed to say, words that might never be spoken otherwise, final thoughts to those who mattered most.

He wrote first to his mom and Allee, his hand stiff from the cold and the exertion. The pen scratched faintly on the paper, each stroke a deliberate effort. He chose his words carefully, aware that the censors would read them and that the Germans might intercept them.

Dearest Mom and Allee,

I'm not at liberty to disclose exactly where I am or what we're doing. They tell us not to, in case these letters fall into the wrong hands, and I understand why. But I want to share what I can, implicitly, so you might appreciate a little of what it's like. It's cold here, colder than any Adirondack winter I've known, and the work... it's unlike anything I've ever experienced.

We've just come through something incredibly difficult—a real climb against formidable obstacles—and we succeeded. However, there is another, even more significant challenge ahead. I can see it from here—a place of intense fire and noise, a constant thunder, and the whispers I hear about what it's costing the others are grim. It's a place that demands everything and more.

I want you to know, Mom, how proud I am of you. For everything you've done, for every sacrifice. For keeping us together, for teaching me to read and count by the firelight, and for creating a home from nothing but grit and love.

And Allee, remember the squirrels and how we would jump from the wood chip piles, learning to get by, always finding a way, even when the woods seemed empty. Hold on to each other, and know that I carry you both with me, a constant warmth in this cold place, always in my thoughts.

I'm not sure when I'll write again. The days ahead are unpredictable, and communication is challenging. Just know that I'm thinking of you, always. And I love you both more than words can say, more than I could ever express.

Love,

Johnnie

He folded the letter carefully, smoothing the creases with his thumb. A lump formed in his throat, which he swallowed hard. Then he took the second piece of paper, his hand trembling slightly, not from the cold but from the raw emotion as he addressed it to Ellie.

Dearest Ellie,

I can't tell you exactly where I am—not in a way that would make sense to you, anyway. But it's cold here, and I'm high up; we've just climbed something no one thought could be climbed—something they called impossible.

I thought of you when we reached the top. Not for any romantic reason at that moment, not with the chaos still ringing in my ears, but because I remembered the way you looked at me the first night we met—as if you were sizing me up as if you could already see what I could be, even if I didn't know it yet. You saw something in me that I hadn't found myself, and you took a leap of faith—believing in me.

That helped me last night, El. More than you know. It kept me going when my legs screamed, and my hands froze. It was a picture of home, a reason to keep climbing.

I wish I could say more. There was snow. There was silence. And then, there wasn't—just noise. But I'm still here. I'm still me. I hope that matters.

Tell your mom how much I miss her apple pie, her hearty potato and bean stew, or even a glass of that sweet cider. And tell your dad that I've told all the guys about the hard cider he makes—the best I've ever tasted.

We've got another mountain ahead. More significant than the last. I don't know when I'll be able to write again. I'm thinking of you, always. And I love you more than words can say, more than I could ever express.

See you at the top,

Johnnie

P.S. That means I love you more.

He sealed both letters. Just as he tucked the letters into his breast pocket Mineo came over, shaking his head. Johnnie wanted to ask, but he didn't.

Mineo solemnly said, "They got Kaminsky."

Johnnie's heart seized. "What happened?"

Mineo's voice was flat, devoid of emotion. "He got hit by a grenade - he's pretty torn up."

As they both stared at the conflagration atop Mount Belvedere, Johnnie, aware of where they might be headed next, said, "He may be one of the lucky ones."

Mineo paused, and then a short, humorless laugh escaped him. "That's what Kaminsky said."

They both shook their heads, a faint, shared smile touching their grim faces.

55

THE LIFELINE

Victory on Riva Ridge was a precarious thing. The summits were theirs, but holding them was another war entirely. The initial assault had relied on speed, stealth, and the sheer audacity of the climb. Sustaining that position, however, required a different kind of miracle—a logistical one.

The pack mules, the backbone of mountain supply, were defeated by the brutal ascent. The poor animals that hauled the 7M1A1 75mm pack howitzers—designed to be broken into mule-loads—to the summit died within hours of reaching it, their hearts giving out from the strain.

The soldiers on the ridge were running desperately low on ammunition, water, and medical supplies. The wounded, stranded on the exposed peak, faced a slow, agonizing wait for evacuation that might never come.

It was into this desperate breach that the men of the 126th Mountain Engineer Battalion stepped. They were a different breed of soldier, their tools not rifles and bayonets, but wrenches, cables, and raw ingenuity. Their task was to build a lifeline—an aerial tramway up the sheer face of Mount Cappel Buso, a steel artery to the heart of the battle.

Johnnie, Mineo, and Luby watched from a relatively secure position as the engineers began their work. It was a feat of impossible courage. Under sporadic but deadly German mortar and sniper fire, two platoons of engineers started the painstaking process of anchoring the tramway to the unforgiving rock.

An incoming howitzer shell screamed overhead, exploding in an airburst that sent white-hot shrapnel hissing into the snow around them. The engineers barely flinched, ducking for a split second before resuming their work, their movements economical.

Johnnie watched in awe, recognizing the unspoken language of shared peril. He was reminded of the quiet, determined competence of the foremen from his CCC days, men who could build a trail or a telephone line through sheer force of will. It was the same focus he'd seen in the eyes of CCC men fighting a forest fire, the same grit he'd felt on the cliffs of Seneca Rocks.

"What's the matter, boys? Never built a ski lift in a shooting gallery before?" a grizzled sergeant barked, a cigar clenched between his teeth. "First time for me, too! Now get that transom in place!"

The engineers moved with a focused, almost serene intensity. They drilled into the rock, the sound a jarring staccato against the backdrop of distant battle. They hauled heavy steel cables, their muscles straining, their faces masks of concentration.

The din of the morning was the clang of steel on steel, the grunt of men heaving two-ton panels into place, and the slow, rhythmic boom of artillery. They were creating something where nothing had existed before, forging a connection between the valley floor and the isolated peak, a bridge of steel and hope.

A young private, straddling a girder to drive a pin home, was suddenly blown from his perch by a nearby mortar blast. Johnnie's breath caught as he tracked the fall, a silent, terrible arc against the white abyss below.

Some men watched with profound sadness. Others turned away and wept. His squadmate, a boy from Ohio with tears mixing with the sweat on his face, didn't even have time to shout. He just kept tightening the bolt, his knuckles white and bleeding.

In eight hours of relentless, death-defying labor, they did it. The Light Tramway M-1 was operational. It was not a grand or elegant structure, but a purely functional machine, a testament to military engineering at its most pragmatic. A simple cable, stretching 1,700 feet and climbing over 600 feet in elevation, with a small, open car suspended beneath it.

The first car that ascended was not filled with men, but with crates of ammunition and cans of water. The sight of it, slowly, steadily making its way up the cliff face, brought a ragged cheer from the exhausted men on the ridge. It was more than just supplies; it was a promise. A promise that they were not alone.

The first car to descend carried two stretchers, each bearing a wounded soldier, their faces pale and still. The tramway cut the evacuation time from a torturous eight-hour journey by litter to less than fifteen minutes—a journey that some medics timed at a miraculous five minutes. It was, quite literally, the difference between life and death.

On its first day of operation, the tramway became the pulsating heart of Riva Ridge. It ferried five tons of supplies to the summit and brought down thirty wounded and twenty dead. It was a constant, rhythmic pulse—ammunition and water ascending, injured and dead descending.

This lifeline did more than just sustain the men on Riva Ridge. This remarkable feat by the 126th Engineers was a lynchpin that secured the ridge, giving the men on Belvedere a vital fighting chance.

LATER THAT DAY, Johnnie, Mineo, and Luby found Kaminsky among the wounded, waiting his turn for the tram. He was pale, his uniform shredded and stained dark with blood, but his eyes were clear.

"Heard you get a chauffeured ride down," Luby said, forcing a grin that didn't quite reach his eyes.

Kaminsky managed a weak, humorless laugh. "Yeah. Guess I'm one of the lucky ones." He looked at the tram, then back at his friends. "You guys... be careful up here."

"We will," Johnnie said, his voice thick. He knelt and clasped Kaminsky's good hand. "See you at the top, buddy."

"Not if I get there first," Kaminsky whispered, the old joke a painful echo of a different time.

They watched as the medics carefully loaded his stretcher onto the tram car. The car began its swaying descent, carrying their friend away from the battle, away from them. They stood in silence, watching until he was just a small, receding shape against the vastness of the valley below.

Johnnie watched the small car moving back and forth, a steady, unwavering presence against the indifferent mountain. The engineers slumped in the mud and snow at the base, their faces smeared with grease and grime. There were no cheers, just exhausted, hollow-eyed grins as they watched their creation work.

It was another kind of trail mark, he thought. Not one of paint on a tree, but one of steel and sweat and unwavering courage, a mark that showed the way not just to the summit, but to survival.

56

THE CALL

21 February 1945

A messenger, grim-faced and mud-splattered, appeared before him, his breath pluming in the cold air. "Staff Sergeant?" the messenger rasped, his voice tight with urgency. "General Hays wants to see you. Immediately. It's about Belvedere."

Johnnie nodded, his gaze fixed on the distant, burning silhouette of Belvedere.

His time had come.

The messenger's words repeated over and over in his head and cut through his heart like a cold blade. He secured his gear, grabbed a fresh coil of rope, and began his rapid descent from Riva Ridge.

The climb up had been brutal, but the rappel down was a controlled fall, a blur of rock and ice, each foot finding purchase with practiced instinct. He moved with a desperate urgency, the distant, muffled thunder of Belvedere's ongoing battle spurring him on.

When he reached the base camp, the scene was a shocking, horrifying departure from the orderly preparations of just a few days prior. What had been a strategic staging ground was now a grim, sprawling open-air hospital and triage unit.

Wounded men, their faces ashen with pain and shock, lay on stretchers, some moaning softly, others utterly silent, awaiting transport to makeshift hospitals further behind the lines. Medics, their uniforms stained with blood and grime, moved with frantic, tireless energy, performing battlefield miracles with what little they had.

Chaplains, their faces etched with profound weariness, knelt beside the dying, offering last rites and quiet comfort. The air hung thick with the metallic tang of blood, the acrid scent of antiseptic, and the pervasive smell of fear.

Johnnie entered the tent, and the man at the center of the storm looked up. This was General Hays. But in that moment, Johnnie saw more than a general. He saw the man from the stories, the one who rode through the storm of steel. He was a living trail mark—a guide who had walked through an inferno and found the path out. And now, he was asking Johnnie to follow that same impossible trail.

General Hays's tent, usually a hub of quiet, strategic planning, was now a crucible of harried desperation. Inside, the air was heavy with cigar smoke and unspoken tension. The officers' faces were drawn and unshaven, their eyes bloodshot from lack of sleep as they hunched over maps, their voices low and strained. Lt. Col. Hampton was there, his usual pragmatic demeanor replaced by a taut wariness.

Hays, a man usually radiating resolute confidence, now carried a visible weight. Hays looked down at the sand table model of Belvedere; his eyes lost focus. This was it. The agonizing day he had carried with him for twenty-seven years. Then, one man had ridden into a storm of steel. Now, he was about to order nearly four-and-a-half thousand of America's finest mountain soldiers to climb into their own inferno, knowing many would not return.

The weight of it was suffocating. He needed a soldier who understood impossible odds. He looked up, his gaze sweeping the room until it fixed onto the one man he knew had already marked an impossible trail. He found Johnnie. "Staff Sergeant," he rasped, his voice hoarse, "glad you could make it." He gestured to a space at the sand table.

"Gentlemen, the situation on Belvedere is critical. The 85th and 87th have fought heroically, securing vital sections of the ridgeline—but they're currently pinned down under intense fire, taking severe casualties. One of the 85th's Battalions has lost over 450 of its 900 men. Enemy artillery continues to decimate any frontal advance. They're running out of ammo and water. Despite our gains on Riva Ridge, the higher ground remains a killing zone."

Hays looked down for a long time at the sand table, which contained a hand-made physical terrain model of Mount Belvedere and the adjacent area constructed to scale using maps and up-to-date aerial photos.

Then he looked up, searching.

Hays's gaze locked onto Johnnie, a flicker of something akin to desperate hope in his tired eyes. "Staff Sergeant," he said, his voice cutting through the tension, "your sharpshooting on Riva Ridge, your speed in reaching that summit...it was exemplary. You blinded them and gave us a crucial opening. You proved that mountain can be taken."

He leaned forward, his voice dropping slightly, an almost pleading tone. "Can you do the same here? Can you find a way for your men to punch through up Belvedere, clear a path, and give us that same advantage?"

A ripple of unease, a silent, shared understanding, passed through the room. Reinforcing the 85th and 87th meant a fresh wave into the meat grinder.

Hays, sensing the unspoken doubt, straightened, attempting to inject a strained optimism into his voice. "The 85th and 87th have bravely softened the approach," he declared, though the words sounded hollow even to his ears, given the fortress at the top.

"They've done their part, drawn fire, and opened some lanes. This isn't a suicide mission; it's a breakthrough waiting to happen." But Johnnie knew it was a desperate gamble.

Johnnie's heart hammered against his ribs.

He took a moment to quickly study the impossible contours on the topographical map, including known enemy emplacements. He clenched his jaw and looked back at General Hays's face, and said, "Yes, Sir. We will do it."

Hays replied, "I knew you could. Thank you, Staff Sergeant. Get your men ready. I'm sending in elements of the 86th to reinforce the 85th."

The words felt like ash in Johnnie's mouth, but he knew there was only one answer. "Yes, sir." After studying the sand table, he did not believe that any soldier could reach the top alive.

Inside, Johnnie began a cold, silent prayer to God for him and his men.

57

THE HEART

Johnnie emerged from General Hays's tent, the heavy canvas flap falling shut behind him, sealing away the stifling air of command and desperation. The cold outside was a shock, but the sight of his men huddled together, their faces etched with anxiety and anticipation, was a familiar anchor.

They had been waiting for him, their eyes fixed on the tent, silently demanding answers. As he approached, a ripple went through the small group, their questions unspoken but clear in their gazes.

"Alright, listen up," Johnnie said, his voice hoarse but firm. He didn't mince words; they deserved the truth or as much of it as he could give. "We're headed to Belvedere. We're going in to join up with some elements of the 85th on the southeast flank."

His announcement was met by a collective intake of breath, a mix of somber nods and subtle shudders. Some faces hardened with quiet resolve, their jaws flexing. Others looked away, a flicker of dread in their eyes, the rumors of Belvedere's carnage visible all around them.

A few muttered curses under their breath. Joining up with

the 85th, they all knew, meant stepping directly into the maw of the beast.

"I know what you're thinking," Johnnie continued, his gaze sweeping over each man, acknowledging their fear without dwelling on it. "But the 85th has softened things up. Our job is to go in, secure what they've gained, and push through."

He paused, letting the weight of the words settle. "Get your affairs in order. Write your letters. Make sure your gear is squared away. We meet back here in one hour. I'll go over the relief plan then, what we know of it."

He dismissed them, watching as they dispersed, their movements heavy with the new burden of the orders. Johnnie himself walked towards the field post, the two letters he'd written earlier heavy in his breast pocket.

He handed them to the weary postal clerk, who nodded gravely, understanding the unspoken finality of such missives. As he turned to leave, a Corporal from the mail detail called out, "Staff Sergeant! I got something for you!"

Johnnie's heart gave a tired thump. He hadn't expected anything. The Corporal handed him two envelopes, one addressed in his mother's familiar, looping script and the other in a precise, almost clinical hand he recognized as Dr. Darby's.

He opened his mother's letter first, his fingers fumbling slightly. The words were like a beautiful view out a window, a glimpse into the quiet world he'd left behind. She wrote about the home front, the persistent cold, and rationing, but mainly about Allee.

My Dearest Johnnie,

It was a great joy to receive your last letter, even though it was brief. We worry about you constantly, but knowing that you're well, even in these difficult circumstances, brings us a measure of peace. The days here are much the same: cold and quiet, but we manage. The garden is still sleeping under the snow, but I'm already planning for spring. Though you probably have new boots now, your old boots are still here by the door, waiting for you.

Allee is doing wonderfully. She's grown into such a capable young woman—remarkable for her age. She's the new Miss Fairchild teaching at the Lake Placid school. She's been a tremendous help with the mending; her stitches are almost as delicate as mine now, and she's taken on much of the heavier work around the house.

She's also quite involved with the Red Cross at the church. She often talks about you and how much she misses your stories from the woods. She even went to town a while back to meet your old friend, now the dashing Lt. Darby, for coffee. Darby wanted to get an update on you; he truly misses you, as we all do.

We still gather by the fire each night, and Allee often reads aloud from the newspaper, which provides the little news we get. We think of you and pray for your safety and that of all the boys. Just keep warm, my son, and know that we are here, waiting. We miss you more than words can express.

All my love, always,
Your Mom

A faint smile touched Johnnie's lips, a brief warmth in the otherwise cold air. Allee was now grown up, teaching and helping. It was a comforting thought, a slice of normalcy. Then he opened Dr. Darby's V-Mail (Victory Mail) message. It was short, just a few lines, typed and almost stark in its brevity. Johnnie read the words, and the world tilted.

It is with the most profound regret that I must inform you of the passing of my son, 2LT Edgar Darby, US Army. He was killed in action on February 2, 1945. He served bravely. We are all heartbroken.

The paper slipped from Johnnie's numb fingers, fluttering to the ground in the snow. Darby. His oldest friend. The boy who taught him how to have fun, who shared his dreams of mountain men and soldiers, who had been his companion since the snowball fight. Gone. Just like that.

A random piece of steel, a world away, had taken him. The cold dread that had settled in his stomach earlier now erupted into a raw, searing pain that tore through him, utterly shattering his composure.

He sank to his knees in the snow, the thunder of Belvedere, a cruel echo of a distant battle that had claimed Darby, his brother in all but blood.

After a while, the searing pain began to dull, replaced by a profound emptiness. Johnnie finally looked up, his eyes gritty, teared-up, unfocused. A chaplain was standing over him, his face grim but kind. His left arm was held close to his body in a crude sling, the end of it a thick, bandaged stump, clearly showing that his left hand was gone and blood was still seeping through.

The chaplain extended his right hand, strong and steady, and said, "Where you headed?" and helped Johnnie back to his feet.

Johnnie told him, "Mt. Belvedere."

The chaplain replied, "May I?"

Johnnie nodded.

The chaplain said, “May the peace of the Lord be with you,” and gave a blessing in the sign of the cross, followed by the same soft salute that Mr. Sandford gave him every morning when he would open the bus door.

Johnnie stared at him in a long silence. He wasn’t looking at the chaplain, though; he was remembering Sundays in that old Lake Placid Episcopal church, the sun streaming through the stained-glass windows, sitting beside his mom and Allee, listening to the hymns, feeling a quiet sense of belonging.

And he remembered what Ellie said about coincidences: "She said they happen when God is smiling at us, a wink - to remind us to have Faith."

Johnnie snapped out of it as the chaplain asked him if he knew the story behind what he was holding in his hand. Johnnie looked down, forgetting what he was holding; instead of his trusty old silver bullet, he noticed he was holding the St. Andrew's Cross.

At that moment, amidst the chaos and grief, he thought of Ellie, and a strange, unexpected peace did indeed come over him—he stared at the Cross for a long time, remembering that last day with her.

He came back to the present and looked up to tell the chaplain about Ellie and how he got the St. Andrew's Cross—but the chaplain had moved away towards Johnnie's men huddled in a group with other soldiers.

Johnnie got up and followed.

58

SERVICE

The air was thick with the smell of courage, fear, and the metallic tang of blood, a grim perfume that clung to their uniforms. Johnnie and his men, along with others, a huddle of weary faces etched with the exhaustion of Riva Ridge and the grim anticipation of Belvedere, stood before Chaplain Hagen.

His uniform, though mud-splattered, seemed to radiate a quiet dignity, and all the soldiers couldn't help but notice that the chaplain's left arm was held in a crude sling, the bandaged stump still seeping blood.

The chaplain looked at them, his eyes holding a profound weariness but also an unwavering light.

"Well, boys," the chaplain began, his voice raspy but clear, "I was planning a proper Sunday service, but it seems you've been a little tied up. Something about kicking Germans off mountains in the middle of the night."

A few tired chuckles rippled through the ranks, a brief, desperate release of tension. "So here we are, Wednesday service. Might not be traditional, but then again, I don't think Jesus and the Apostles kept a strict schedule either."

He paused, then grew serious, his gaze sweeping - to look into the eyes of each man. "You climbed cliffs in the dark, in silence, knowing full well what might be waiting at the top. That's not just bravery; that's sacrifice. That's service. It reminds me of someone else who climbed toward danger for the sake of others."

He looked at Johnnie, a flicker of recognition in his eyes and their earlier conversation.

“You know," the chaplain continued, walking towards Johnnie, his voice softening, "that cross you're wearing, the saltire, that's St. Andrew's Cross. St. Andrew was one of Jesus' first followers—a fisherman who dropped his nets when he was called. He didn't fight as a soldier. Didn't command armies. But he went. Far from home. Into foreign lands. Greece, Scythia—places that didn't speak his tongue, didn't share his customs, didn't believe in his God. He went not to take, but to give. To free people, not from soldiers, but from fear and despair. He defied the old ways and established norms because he knew that a greater truth demanded a new path. Sometimes, boys, the path to salvation, or even just survival, isn't the one laid out for you. Sometimes, you have to forge a new one, one that defies what everyone else believes."

The chaplain's eyes were steady, reflecting a profound, ancient wisdom.

"In the end, the Romans caught him. Told him to stop preaching. He wouldn't. So they nailed him to a cross, but not like Jesus'. Andrew said he wasn't worthy of that. So they made him a diagonal cross—an ‘X’—similar to the mark you wear now, the crossed bayonets on your 10th Mountain Patch."

He nodded towards the cross.

"St. Andrew died with strangers watching. But they saw something in him—courage, mercy, peace. Something of Christ." He rested his good hand on Johnnie's shoulder, a firm, comforting pressure.

"Now here you all are. A long way from home. Facing death not for land or glory, but to free people you've never met. Sounds a lot like Andrew. The world might never know your name, but heaven already does."

He paused, then continued, "That 10th Mountain cross on your chest—it's not just a mark of sacrifice. It means someone came this way before... and someone greater walks with you still."

The chaplain then closed his eyes, his voice rising, a solemn prayer echoing in the frigid air.

"Almighty God, we stand before you, humble, weary, yet resolute. We ask for strength for these men as they face the trials on Mount Belvedere. Grant them courage in the face of fear, clarity in the chaos, and unwavering purpose in their mission. Protect them, Lord, from the unseen dangers and the enemy's fury. May their steps be guided, their aim be true, and their resolve unyielding. Watch over their families, far from this battle-scarred land, and bring them safely home. Amen."

A solemn chorus of "Amen" rippled through the ranks, a unified, quiet vow.

59

THE SQUIRRELS

The order to move out for Belvedere arrived swiftly, a blunt and unyielding command that jolted Johnnie's squad—twelve battle-weary soldiers of the 86th—from their brief, uneasy rest at the base. They were being committed to the inferno, tasked with reinforcing and attempting to break the deadly stalemate.

As they began their approach towards the Belvedere sector, where the 85th was heavily engaged, the ground grew more treacherous—a deceptive mix of icy patches, slick mud churned by explosions, and deep snow drifts 4-5 feet high.

The air, thin and biting, grew heavy with the metallic tang of ever closer explosions and the nearing, sharper crackle of machine-gun fire that seemed to claw at the edges of their hearing.

Johnnie's men, bone-weary from their days of battle on and around Riva Ridge and now burdened by grim rumors and the visible evidence of decimated squads from the 85th and 87th being brought back, shuffled forward.

Their movements were leaden, faces drawn and pale under layers of grime, eyes wide with exhaustion and raw fear.

The crushing weight of their 75-pound fighting load, a steel-framed mountain rucksack, the relentless cold seeping into their marrow, and the chilling knowledge of the hell ahead—the very 'ring of fire' they had witnessed consuming their comrades—pressed down on them, a tangible burden.

Johnnie felt their apprehension like a physical presence, a bitter taste in the frigid air, a palpable tension that crackled around them, mirroring the knot of dread in his gut.

He saw Private Miller stumble, not from the terrain, but as if the sheer weight of the oncoming barrage was a physical blow.

He knew that a direct order to push on, to follow the same brutal paths that'd stalled other brave men, simply wouldn't be enough, not now, not after what they'd already endured and what they now faced.

Darby was gone. His letter, with its stark warning about *routine* becoming a "positive danger" in war, now echoed with urgent clarity.

Mr. Sandford—his father—and the silent, poisonous cloud of mustard gas that had killed anyone trapped inside lingered in his thoughts.

Then the chaplain's words returned: *Sometimes the path to survival isn't the one already laid out for you.*

But most of all, there was Ellie. The St. Andrew's Cross. Her words about faith.

He closed his eyes and prayed.

He saw her—her smile, the curve of her lips—and then he heard her voice as if she were right beside him: "*Find your way back to me, Johnnie Grey.*"

Darby's warning clashed with every instinct. The ring of fire ahead felt like a suffocating trap, no different from the gas cloud that had taken his father. But now, the chaplain's challenge to forge new paths merged with Ellie's unwavering faith—crystallizing into a single, terrifying thought:

What if the most direct path—the one that looked suicidal—was their only chance?

And it began to dawn on him—a tickle at first, then a thought, then an epiphany.

He and his men needed to set aside training and instinct to run straight through Kesselring's 'ring of fire' and reach the heart at the summit.

They needed to take a leap of faith.

It was their best chance at survival. He took another deep breath, the cold air burning his lungs, and then, with a sudden, decisive clarity born of desperation and memory, he raised a gloved hand, signaling a halt.

"Alright, everybody, stop. Huddle up."

His voice, though hoarse, carried a quiet authority that demanded attention.

Relief, brief but palpable, rippled through the ranks as they gratefully sank into the snow, forming a tight circle around him. Their breath plumed in cold, misty clouds.

Before Johnnie could speak, he heard a muffled sob from the rear, quickly stifled. Another soldier, young Henderson, dropped his rifle in the snow, his hands shaking too violently to retrieve it immediately.

Their eyes, when they met Johnnie's, were not just demanding answers but pleading for a reprieve, any reprieve, from the hell that awaited.

Johnnie took a deep breath, the cold air stinging his lungs, and slowly exhaled. "Listen," he began, his voice low and almost conversational, a distinct change from the distant din of the battle.

“Back home in the Adirondacks, things were tough-especially during the Depression. My family and I didn't have much. So, my job from the time I was a little kid was to hunt, mostly squirrels.”

A few tired chuckles rippled through the group, a

surprising sound in the grim landscape. "Squirrels, huh, Staff Sergeant?" someone jibed, a faint grin breaking through the grime on his face.

Johnnie nodded, a faint, distant smile touching his lips, a memory of a different kind of struggle. "Yeah, squirrels. Red ones, mostly. Fast little bastards, I tell you. Nimble. Smart. I spent hours out there, learning their ways and watching how they moved. How they stay alive when everything else wants to eat 'em - hawks, foxes, even us."

He paused, letting the image settle in their minds; the simplicity of the hunt was a profound contrast to the complex, deadly war around them.

“I had this one prized steel ball bearing. I found it years ago. I'd killed sixty-three cottontail rabbits with that single piece of steel. Rabbits are a tough shot with a slingshot, much harder than squirrels.”

The men listened, captivated. The story, so far removed from their present hell, offered a strange, unexpected comfort, a brief mental escape. Many nodded in recognition of a shared history of hardship and resourcefulness.

"My old man used to hunt rabbits for stew," one soldier offered, his voice thick with nostalgia. "Deer, for us," another added, "when we were lucky enough to find one."

The shared memory of what was now seen as simpler times—hunting for survival instead of being hunted—created a brief, unexpected bond, a common thread woven through their disparate lives.

"Now, here's the kicker about those squirrels," Johnnie continued, his voice shifting and taking on a deeper, more serious tone. A focused intensity now replaced the playful glint in his eye.

"When you hunt a squirrel, they don't run in a straight line. They zig, then stop dead, then sprint off in a completely different direction. They zig-zag forward, sideways, backward, then stop, and then move forward again. It makes them unpredictable for aimed fire, right? The hunter can't lead the shot if he doesn't know where the target's going next. That's instinct, and against a single hunter or a hawk, it's a lifesaver. It's a survivor's dance. But what happens when that squirrel isn't dodging one threat but an entire, unavoidable hailstorm or trying to cross a wide, busy road? That same zig-zag keeps them in the danger zone longer."

Mineo, noticing Luby smirking to himself, nudged him. "Alright, Luby, spit it out. What's so funny?" Luby, ever ready, muttered, "It helps you make roadkill stew, though."

A few men managed a weary chuckle at Luby's remark, the dark humor a momentary distraction. Still, Johnnie pressed on, his eyes sweeping over them.

"But this isn't aimed fire, boys. Not here. Not this 'ring of fire.' This is saturation. We took out most of their eyes on Riva Ridge; they can't see us. They're mostly just blanketing the entire area with shells, an indiscriminate hail of steel. They're not aiming at you. They're aiming at this ground, creating a 'ring of fire,' hoping we're stupid enough to spend time zigging, zagging, crawling, or dodging. Every second we spend in the ring increases our chances of a random piece of shrapnel finding us. Zig-zagging actually increases our exposure time in this kind of bombardment because it slows us down. It's like a rainstorm - the longer you're out there, the wetter you get."

He paused, letting the grim truth sink in.

"Rolf Monsen, my old ski instructor, always said the secret to being a great skier was falling—pushing your limits, finding new ways. Later, at Seneca Rocks, we learned about holding on —knowing your limits and trusting your grip.

But my best friend Darby wrote me a letter once, and his point stuck with me. All our training, all the drills—they build routine. That's the whole idea. Out here, though, where everything's trying to kill us, routine can get us killed.

Our instinct is to zig-zag, stay low, keep moving, take cover. We've been taught that. But on this terrain, in these conditions, that instinct is a death trap. The rules are different here—and if we don't adapt, we won't make it.

This ring of fire isn't a hunter taking a single shot. It's the sky raining shrapnel, chewing up the ground and anyone on it. Every zig, every zag—while we try to dodge what can't be dodged—just gives those random fragments more time to find us."

He gestured to a young Private Miller, fresh-faced and still trembling slightly from the cold and fear.

"Miller! You. Sprint for that tree, and back, like a squirrel, fast as you can."

The soldier, surprised but eager to obey, sprang up and dashed off in a jerky, unpredictable sequence of starts, stops, and sudden changes in direction.

The others watched, a genuine if brief, moment of levity, the sound echoing strangely in the quiet before Belvedere.

Then Miller tagged the tree and began his "squirrel run" back. As he ran, Johnnie timed him and counted out loud - one one thousand, two, three, four, five, and so on to eleven seconds.

Johnnie rose, his own weary body moving with a sudden, decisive purpose. Time me.

Then, men counted out as he took long strides, accelerating into a strong, unwavering sprint, his eyes fixed on the distant tree that Miller had tagged earlier.

He ran straight, powerfully, covering the ground with maximum efficiency, then stopped abruptly, tagged the tree, and ran straight back at full speed, his breath pluming in the cold air. Five seconds.

"This," he panted, his voice ringing with conviction, "is our new instinct. This is how we survive this fire. We don't zig-zag. We don't try to outsmart a random barrage. We get out of it.

Fast. Straight. Every man, as fast as his legs can carry him, from here to the German bunkers. Minimize exposure. That's the only way through this."

Then Luby let out a soft chuckle to himself, a sound that seemed to defy the grim reality. Mineo, sensing the impending quip, urged, 'C'mon, Luby, out with it,' a flicker of a smile on his face.

Luby paused a mischievous sparkle in his eye. He looked at Johnnie, then at the huddled, exhausted men.

"What you're saying is..." Luby paused again, drawing out the words, "... we're fucking squirrels who run straight."

A beat of stunned silence, then a collective, explosive burst of laughter ripped through the ranks, a raw, desperate release of tension that echoed strangely in the quiet before Belvedere. Johnnie laughed long and hard, too, the sound almost painful in its relief.

When the laughter finally subsided, Mineo shook his head, a genuine smile on his face. "I never heard him swear before." They laughed again because the running joke of Luby and Mineo, the old married couple, continued to live on, even here.

Then, Johnnie paused, the humor draining from his face, replaced by a fierce, unyielding resolve that hardened his features. The silence stretched uncomfortably long, broken only by the distant thud of artillery from Belvedere that brought them back.

His voice rang with a conviction that cut through the cold and the fear—a voice weighted by loss and burning with the raw hope of survival. "Yes," he said.

"We are squirrels. We are the fucking squirrels of the 10th Mountain Division of the United States of America. And we're going to run straight through that ring of fire and take out every last German at the top."

To a man, their faces hardened. Shoulders that had been slumped with dread now straightened. Fear was eclipsed by a grim, shared determination that seemed to spark a fire in the frigid air, a defiant glint in their eyes.

A single, powerful word—a collective vow—resonated through the ranks: a promise to themselves, to each other, and the mountain they were about to assault.

A unified 'Amen' ripped through the huddled men, a silent pact sealing their resolve.

60

THE SNOWBALL FIGHT - PART II

21 February 1945

At 2300 hours, under cover of darkness, Johnnie and his squad began their climb into the sector of Mount Belvedere that elements of the 85th were holding.

As they got closer to the summit, Johnnie's earlier lesson resonated—instead of slowing down, they accelerated.

From the outside, under the eerie flicker of flares and the crackle of weapons fire that briefly illuminated their frantic scramble, he and his men looked like a scattered group of driven, migrating squirrels, dashing relentlessly forward, carving a straight line through the chaos.

The men gathered themselves - and began their run.

They sprinted through bursts of machine guns fired aimlessly in the dark, drove straight through hidden craters, and dashed as fast as they could; their movements formed a desperate, unwavering charge against the constant, murderous rain of German artillery fire.

They moved not as trained soldiers but as primal creatures, their bodies reacting faster than their minds could process, seeking refuge through sheer, unyielding speed, driven directly by the shortest route through the danger.

And then, for Johnnie, it got quiet.

All he could hear was the sound of his breath—*inhale*. His boots lunged up the steep mountainside, and with each stride —*exhale*—his lungs were tested—, and they held—forged by years of hard work—*inhale*: hiking, climbing, skiing through thin, high-altitude mountain air—*exhale*.

The 75-pound combat rucksack on his back bounced with every step of his powerful legs, driving upward—*inhale*—through the silence, through the fire—*exhale*. Breathing in—*inhale*—pushing out—*exhale*—propelled forward by the rhythm of survival.

On the inside, for Johnnie, the world began to narrow, and the chaos of Belvedere—the inferno of war—receded. The thunder of the howitzers faded, replaced by the shouts of children, the crisp crack of snowballs, and the distant, melodic peal of a church bell—*inhale*. He wasn't running straight up an impossible climb; his mind was charging straight down the snow-covered streets of Lake Placid

The cold air stung his cheeks with an exhilarating bite, a pile of snowballs clutched in his shirt pouch—*exhale*. Beside him, a phantom presence was Darby, his face alight with mischievous glee, his laughter echoing in the crisp winter air.

Ahead, at the end of Main Street, the foreign adults from the Olympics, a formidable wall of figures, converged, blocking his path. Behind them, he saw her, Ellie—*inhale*. Her brown hair tied back with a ribbon, a few stray tendrils framing her face. Her eyes, a warm, deep brown—*exhale*. He could feel the St. Andrew's Cross, its weight against his chest, a tangible promise he had to keep.

He was driving straight through, a blur of motion, eyes locked on the imagined path beyond the ranks—*inhale*—trying to break through that wall of men—*exhale*. His speed and these sharp, vivid images in his mind were his trail marks—a sacred protection from the present horror, a momentary reprieve from the brutal reality of Belvedere.

In this fragile mental sanctuary, he could still feel the warmth of friendship, the lightness of youth, and his deep love for Ellie, fueling his relentless push.

They ran on in the dark—*inhale*—straight past exploding craters, up frozen gullies, past the shattered bodies of their brothers in the 10th who the Germans had killed—*exhale*—racing their way toward the summit, each step a desperate lunge, a testament to sheer will, a refusal to yield.

As Johnnie's squad, employing their 'straight run' tactic, punched through the outer edges of the ring of fire and neared the main German bunker complexes near the top—*inhale*—the relentless howitzer fire targeting their immediate path began to thin, then stopped altogether.

THE GERMANS WOULDN'T CALL in their heaviest artillery strikes too close to their hardened bunkers; they risked killing themselves with their own shells.

They had reached the German main line of resistance, the fortified heart of Belvedere in this sector. This was where the real test began, where the war of evasion through the artillery storm ended, and the war of annihilation by rifle, grenade, and bayonet started.

Johnnie snapped out of it. Shrill, piercing blasts of noise hammered his eardrums. The laughter and innocence of his boyhood dreams vanished, replaced by the chilling reality of the mountain's summit defenses—a grim, jagged silhouette of concrete, barbed wire, and steel against the pre-dawn sky. This was no game.

This was close-quarters, brutal combat. Kill or be killed. War.

Here, the men of Johnnie's company, now fighting alongside soldiers of the 85th and supported by the continued pressure from the 87th on other parts of the mountain, crashed against the German defenses.

It was a convergence of effort, a desperate, unified push by all three regiments of the 10th Mountain Division to break the enemy's grip.

Johnny prayed, whispering to God, "Our Father ...," as he ran into the maelstrom. The air was thick with the shouts of men, the metallic clang of bayonets against flesh and steel, the guttural cries of Germans defending their last strongholds, and the desperate screams of the wounded.

Johnnie and his men, alongside their comrades, engaged in the most brutal hand-to-hand combat, a hopeless, feudal struggle for every inch of high ground.

They threw grenades into pillboxes, the concussive blasts echoing inside the concrete, followed by the sickening thud of bodies.

They cleared bunkers with bayonets, their movements precise and ruthless, driven by the primal need to survive and to avenge their fallen comrades. The fighting was a maelstrom, a testament to the sheer will of men pushed beyond their limits, a desperate, bloody dance of death.

After hours of brutal, close-quarters fighting, with heavy losses on both sides, the combined pressure of the 85th, 86th, and 87th Regiments began to shatter the German defenses on the main Belvedere-Gorgolesco ridgeline.

The fighting, however, was far from over.

German counterattacks came hard and often in the days and nights that followed. It wasn't until 24 February that the 10th Mountain Division finally secured the entire Mount Belvedere—Gorgolesco complex, breaking Kesselring's grip on the high ground—and opening the path for the Fifth Army to push north.

JUST BEFORE DAWN, on a cold Sunday morning, 25 February 1945, the American flag was raised on a charred pole by weary but triumphant soldiers. It stood as a defiant beacon against the gray sky, a symbol of the incredible courage and sacrifice of all the men of the 10th Mountain Division who had fought for this critical ground.

Below them, scattered amidst the wreckage of their defenses, the Germans began to raise white flags, their resistance finally broken, their spirit crushed.

Johnnie sat beside a steaming foxhole or crater, he didn't know which, helmet in his lap, his hands too numb to shake, too cold to feel anything but the dull ache of existence.

Around him, medics moved from body to body, their movements grim and methodical, their faces etched with the profound weariness of their task, their eyes holding the unspeakable horrors they had witnessed.

The mountain was theirs—but the cost had been steep, etched in blood and loss, in the silent, still forms that lay scattered across the snow, forever part of Belvedere.

Lt. Col. Hampton arrived on top, his face drawn with exhaustion, his uniform torn in places, stopping just long enough to pat Johnnie's shoulder. "You did good, kid. We all did. You got us through that hellfire."

Johnnie didn't answer. His thoughts were far away—on Darby, whose memory had unknowingly guided his steps through the storm, whose spirit had danced beside him in the face of death. On Ellie, waiting unknowingly at home, a fragile hope in a world of despair.

61

AFTER THE SUMMIT

The sun slowly rose over Mount Belvedere, casting long, broken shadows over the battle-scarred landscape, revealing the full extent of the devastation. The silence was eerie—less peace, more the absence of screaming, a hollow echo of the violence that had just passed, a void where the sound should have been.

There was no parade. No cheers. Just nods—tight-lipped, knowing. The kind of nods only soldiers give each other when they've seen the worst, faced the abyss, and are still breathing, a silent brotherhood forged in fire and blood.

A chaplain, his uniform dusty, said prayers over a row of poncho-covered shapes, their forms heartbreakingly still, their sacrifice a silent testament to the fallen. A few soldiers bowed their heads, their silent pleas sent skyward, their faith a fragile comfort.

That night, the commanders permitted a fire—just one. A small, single flame flickered in a crater, its warmth a welcome comfort against the brutal cold, a tiny beacon in the vast darkness.

Around it, men gathered, sipping weak, bitter coffee from

tin cups, their hands trembling slightly, passing around a shared bottle of something substantial and nameless. The liquid burned a welcome path down their throats, dulling the edges of their pain.

No one spoke of the fight, not yet. The words were too heavy, too raw, too fresh.

Johnnie sat with Mineo and Luby and the few others who remained of their squad; the empty spaces around them were a painful reminder of who was missing, of the friends they had lost. Mineo stared into the dancing flames, his face a mask of exhaustion, his eyes haunted.

"I thought it'd feel better," he finally said, his voice raspy, barely a whisper, the words hanging in the air.

"It does," Johnnie replied after a long pause, the words tasting raw in his mouth, a bitter truth. "Just not the kind of better we hoped for."

Behind them, the American flag swayed—proof that they'd done the impossible. That they'd climbed what couldn't be climbed. That they'd won.

But beneath it, in the silence between breaths, lay the heavy, undeniable weight of what they'd lost to do it.

62

THE FINAL PUSH

Time accelerated, a dizzying rush toward the inevitable end. The war, a wounded titan, was finally collapsing. Stripped of their high ground and shattered strategic advantage, the Germans were in retreat, their disciplined lines crumbling under the relentless pressure of the U.S. Fifth Army and the 10th Mountain Division's unyielding assault. The tide had irrevocably turned.

As they prepared to advance into the vast, open plains of the Po Valley, so different from the unforgiving mountains they had just conquered, Johnnie briefed his men, just as Rolf used to, illustrating tactical maneuvers with a stick drawn in the dirt instead of snow, his voice calm and steady against the surrounding chaos.

They joked about Hannibal and his 37 war elephants crossing the Alps, a gallows humor that masked their grim determination.

Johnnie mused, "Think what it must have taken for Hannibal, back in 218 BC, to get his army and all those war elephants over these mountains to try and conquer the Romans."

Mineo chimed in, "All it would take is a hundred thousand

men—strong men with determination." They all turned to look at Luby, who was smirking. Mineo sighed. "Out with it."

Luby replied, "Or just a few men with huge bags of peanuts."

They got it, and a ripple of laughter went through the men.

Luby held up his hands in mock innocence. "What? I meant they could leave a trail of peanuts for the elephants." He smirked, a twinkle in his eye. "...what did you think I meant?"

The laughter, like the spring ice, slowly faded away. The mountains were behind them. Ahead lay the valley and the final chase.

63

THE CHASE

The Po Valley was a world away from the frozen hell of the Apennines. The air, thick and humid, hung heavy with the scent of damp earth and blooming spring, a stark contrast to the sharp, sterile cold of the high peaks.

But the war here was no less brutal. It was a different kind of fight—a war of relentless pursuit. The 10th Mountain Division, having advanced over 75 miles in just eight and a half days, was moving with a speed that left the Germans reeling.

On 20 April, Major General George P. Hays ordered the formation of Task Force Duff—a powerful combined arms unit including tanks, tank-destroyers, engineers, and infantry.

Beginning at 0630 hours on 21 April, the 10th's Task Force Duff spearheaded the Fifth Army's rapid dash north toward the Po River, requisitioning every available vehicle to maintain their relentless momentum.

By nightfall, they had seized the bridge over the Panaro River at the town of Bomporto, after the engineers had quickly removed the explosive charges the Germans had placed under the bridge.

The advance was a relentless blur of motion across the flatlands. The landscape became a chaotic canvas of burning fields and the grim detritus of a retreating army.

Allied planes owned the skies, pounding enemy convoys and leaving destroyed German tanks and vehicles lining the highways, their metal hulls twisted and blackened. Thousands of German troops streamed southward as captives, while others, surrounded, abandoned vast quantities of equipment in their desperate flight.

On 22 April, the German 90th Panzer Grenadier Division, once seemingly invincible, was now in full retreat—a wounded beast fleeing for the perceived safety of the Alps. The 10th Mountain Division, now the spearhead of the Fifth Army, was hot on their heels.

"They're running for the Po," Lt. Col. Hampton briefed them, his voice raw with exhaustion, his finger tracing a wide, muddy river on the map. "If they make it across, they can regroup, dig in, and we'll have another bloody stalemate. We can't let that happen."

The Germans reached the Po River first, a 200 to 300-yard-wide, brown serpent of water that promised salvation. But the bridges were gone, destroyed by their own engineers or shattered by Allied bombs. For the Panzer division, it was a dead end.

Johnnie and his squad arrived at the riverbank second, to a scene of chaos. German soldiers were abandoning their heavy equipment, stripping off uniforms, and plunging into the cold, swift current in a desperate swim for survival.

"Well, I'll be," Luby muttered, watching the scene unfold from afar. "It's the German swim team."

The order came down the line: "Assault boats! We're crossing!"

On 23 April, at noon, the 10th began its crossing of the Po in assault boats. The 126th Engineer boat crews launched their flotilla, comprising storm boats, rafts, and DUKWs—

amphibious trucks nicknamed "Ducks" that could be used as boats—churning the brown water.

Johnnie's shoulders burned as he and his men paddled their raft with furious energy, the cold spray of the Po slapping their faces. The air was a disorienting hell of whumping artillery, cracking rifles, and panicked shouts in two languages.

The 10th, the first American division to cross the Po, hit the northern bank, scrambling ashore into the thick mud. The fight for the riverbank was short and brutal. The Germans, having abandoned their heavy weapons, were outgunned and overwhelmed. The path to the Alps was open, clearing the way for the final push toward Germany.

Once they were across, the chaos of the river crossing gave way to a different kind of fight. The war of pursuit became a war of endurance—a grueling, seemingly endless hike northward. The rhythm of the march was a monotonous, soul-crushing drumbeat against the packed earth. For Johnnie, a man made for woods, snow, and incline, the open flatland was unnerving; the lack of high ground felt like a missing limb.

"My sore feet have sore feet," Mineo groaned one afternoon, collapsing onto the side of the road and pulling off a boot to inspect a new blister.

"No complaints here," Luby retorted, though his face was etched with a deep weariness. "At least we're not getting shot at every five minutes."

It was true. The skirmishes were fewer, the work of a broken force, designed to delay, not to win. They had been marching for what felt like days when, ahead, a small, battered German half-track struggled to cross a makeshift bridge. Johnnie raised a hand, signaling a halt. Through his binoculars, he saw a handful of German soldiers, their faces etched with exhaustion and despair.

"They're done," Johnnie said, his voice flat. "No fight left."

"So, we just walk up and take 'em?" Mineo asked, a hint of disbelief in his tone.

"That's the new war, Mineo," Johnnie replied. "They run, we chase. They break, we capture. No more digging in, no more holding lines. Just... forward."

Luby smirked. "I like this new war."

Mineo couldn't help himself. "Why?"

Luby's smirk vanished, replaced by a gravity they rarely saw. "Because the last war I was in," he said slowly, "was like climbing to the top of the Empire State Building with a 75-pound rucksack on my back. In the dark. On ice. With people at the top trying to kill me."

A stunned silence fell over the group. Johnnie's eyes met Luby's, and he saw the profound truth of it. "Amen," Johnnie murmured, and the others echoed him, the word a shared, solemn understanding.

THE HIKE CONTINUED, each mile a small victory. As they took a brief halt on the road to Lake Garda in late April 1945, the air thick with the smell of diesel and spring, Lt. Col. Hampton's jeep pulled up beside them. He looked even more exhausted than they were.

"Grey," Hampton called out, his voice hoarse. He hopped out and walked over to Johnnie. "The final reports on Belvedere are making the rounds. Your 'straight run'... they're calling it decisive. General Hays personally cited your leadership in breaking the line and getting us across the Po."

He pulled a set of Technical Sergeant stripes from his pocket and pressed them into Johnnie's hand. "This is for Riva Ridge, for Belvedere, for this whole damn chase. You're leading these men to the finish line. Make it official." He gave Johnnie a firm clap on the shoulder, then got back in his jeep and sped off toward the front.

Johnnie looked at the stripes in his palm, then at the weary faces of his men. There was still one more fight to come.

As they pushed deeper into the Alpine foothills, their momentum became unstoppable, racing against Mussolini's downfall and the collapse of the Axis in Italy. The final objective, Lake Garda, was now within reach.

The chase finally cornered the enemy at the northern shores of Lake Garda. There, in a last, desperate stand, the Germans turned to fight. The battle for the towns of Torbole and Riva del Garda, and the defiant fortress of Monte Brione that loomed over them, was the final, brutal test. After it fell, the 10th had sealed the last road to the Brenner Pass.

With the Brenner Pass secured, the last major supply artery for the German war machine in Italy—including its critical fuel pipeline—was severed. All remaining Axis formations south of the Alps were now trapped.

With no fuel, no supplies, and no routes left for retreat, the estimated one million Axis soldiers and personnel in Italy had two choices: ditch their weapons and surrender in place, or be annihilated in pockets. They chose the former, and Italy's war ended on 2 May.

After 114 days of continuous battle, the fight was over. For Johnnie, Luby, and Mineo, who had survived it all, Italy was finally free.

~

64

LAKE GARDA

May 1945

The way the mountains ran down to the shore reminded Johnnie of his home in Lake Placid. He sat for a long time, his gaze fixed on the shimmering expanse of the lake. Its surface was indifferent to the tragedy that had unfolded, reflecting only the rich blue Italian sky. The breeze moved through the grass, a soft, uncaring sigh, carrying away the echoes of his shattered grief.

He clasped the cross Ellie had given him, its chain still resting against his throat, letting it swing gently between his fingers. The metal warmed by the sun offered a fragile comfort, a tangible piece of her, a world now impossibly distant. He traced its intricate beauty, dreaming of her laughter and the warmth of her embrace.

He reached into his pocket, his fingers finding the familiar, smooth sphere wrapped in a tattered cloth. He unwrapped his prized silver bullet from its tattered cloth pouch, the polished metal a poignant symbol of innocence lost, of a life that felt a million miles away.

He thought about Darby. He thought about Allee, Dr. and Mrs. Darby. He thought about how much they all had lost.

"See you up top," he whispered, the words ragged, torn from his throat, lost to the wind as he skipped the steel ball like a stone into the lake, retiring it, thanking it for helping him put food on the table and helping him learn how to survive. He would never use it to kill again.

65

VICTORY

The war in Italy ended. The announcement of the unconditional surrender of German Army Group C came over the radio on 2 May, a broadcast confirming what the men on the ground already knew: the enemy was defeated. The fighting was over.

For Johnnie, Mineo, and Luby, bivouacked in a temporary camp near the waters of Lake Garda, the quiet waiting in a foreign place felt heavier than any rucksack. They were victors, but they felt more like survivors, standing on the edge of a world still far from home.

Then news of the final, total German surrender arrived on 7 May. The announcer's voice spoke of wild celebrations in Times Square, of strangers kissing in the streets of London. But in their small circle, the announcement of Victory in Europe —'V-E Day'—was met with cheers held in check by a weariness as they awaited new orders.

They passed around a bottle of grappa, the glass warm from their hands. They drank to the victory and to the men who weren't there to share it. For Darby. For Kaminsky. For the faces and names that would forever be etched into the rock of Riva

Ridge and the slopes of Belvedere. For the men who fell in the Po Valley and at the foot of the Alps in the final days of the battle.

"So, what now?" Mineo asked, his voice rough. He stared into the fire as if searching for an answer in the flames.

"Now," Luby said, his usual smirk absent, "we wait for the other shoe to drop."

Johnnie looked at the faces of his friends, illuminated by the flickering firelight. No one spoke, but the same thought was reflected in their eyes—that other shoe had a name: Japan.

The war in Europe was over, but the global conflict continued to rage.

The rumor, soon confirmed by orders, was that the 10th was slated for redeployment to the Pacific—a beachhead landing on D-Day plus one near Yokohama. From there, they would fight their way into the mountains surrounding Tokyo.

The thought of it was a heavy weight in the pit of Johnnie's stomach. He held the St. Andrew's Cross in his hand and prayed. He had survived one front. Could he do it again?

Then more news arrived, first in hushed, hopeful whispers and then in fragmented reports over the radio, the signal struggling to break through the static. A bomb, they said, but that wasn't the right word. They spoke of a single weapon that had erased a city called Hiroshima, of a fire brighter than the sun.

The men, who understood war in terms of feet on the ground and the bark of a rifle, couldn't grasp it. "One bomb?" Mineo had asked, shaking his head in disbelief. "How?"

When news of a second city, Nagasaki, followed, the disbelief curdled into a terrifying awe. Six days after the second bomb, on 15 August 1945, Emperor Hirohito announced Japan's surrender, his voice a foreign and disembodied sound that traveled across the world.

The war was over—all of it. The words hung in the air, too

large to comprehend. Luby let out a long, slow breath he seemed to have been holding since Riva Ridge.

A sudden, unbelievable peace fell over the world. There would be no invasion of Japan. No new mountains to climb. The orders for the Pacific were rescinded. They were going home.

That night, the weariness finally broke. It was a celebration of roaring cheers. Men drank, danced, and shouted praise at the stars above. Harmonicas played, and guitars, too. Mineo, tears streaming down his face, laughed until he couldn't breathe. They built the bonfire so high that the sparks seemed to join the stars. It was a night of pure joy, a wild surrender to the hope they had carried deep within them for so long, but for which they refused to allow to come to the surface.

By November 1945, the 10th Mountain Division, having fulfilled its unique purpose and accomplished its mission, was deactivated.

The men of the 10th were going home, forever marked by the trails they had blazed and the brothers they had left behind. They were returning to a world that celebrated the victory but could never fully understand what they had done to achieve it.

66

HOME

Autumn 1945

Lake Placid seemed like the logical place to go, the mountains of his youth, the familiar faces, the comforting routines. He would get there soon. But Johnnie found that logic had little to do with love or with the deep, quiet ache in his soul.

Instead, on a cold morning with leaves just beginning to turn in the golden hills of West Virginia—a landscape that felt both new and strangely familiar—Johnnie Grey stepped off a bus in Elkins.

His uniform was worn, faded by sun and rain, and now bore a few more ribbons than when he'd left. His duffel bag was slung over one shoulder, skis lashed crosswise, symbols of his past and a hint of his future.

He walked the familiar dirt road to Ellie's farm, his boots kicking up dust with each step, a silent prayer on his lips. His heart pounded a rhythm stronger than any drum, a mixture of anticipation and fear.

She was outside, pinning laundry in the crisp breeze, her back to him, her figure breathtaking and familiar against the vastness of the fields.

She looked up, perhaps sensing his presence or merely catching a shift in the air, a subtle disturbance in the quiet morning. Their eyes met across the yard, and in that instant, the world narrowed to just the two of them.

Neither said a word. There was no need.

The silence stretched, vast and profound, filled instead with the tremor in his hands, the sudden blur of tears in her eyes, and the desperate, overwhelming pull that drew them together.

She dropped the clothespins, scattering them across the grass like tiny, fallen petals, and sprinted across the yard, her arms wide, her face alight with a joy that seemed to banish the very shadows, throwing herself into his embrace.

He held her close, burying his face in her hair, breathing in the scent of her, of home, of everything he had fought for and almost lost.

After the longest embrace, Johnnie took the St. Andrew's Cross from around his neck and placed it back on Ellie. He whispered in her ear, holding her tight, tears of joy. "You are my tenth trail mark—you brought me home."

THE BROKEN SKIS FROM CHILDHOOD, lovingly repaired, found their place over the fire in their fireplace, a silent arc of wood mirroring the circle his life had turned. His old, handmade slingshot, the ashwood dark with age and oil, rested on their mantelpiece - a quiet, profound miracle of life preserved.

And the mountain, finally, was still. Its echoes had faded, replaced by the gentle rhythms of home. He had survived the mountains of Europe, the brutal, echoing peaks of war, and returned to the quiet, familiar mountains of home to the woman who had waited for him.

He was no longer a boy with a slingshot.

He was a mountain soldier.

AUTHOR'S NOTE - PART II

Field Marshal Kesselring's Gothic Line

Riva Ridge and the three peaks - Belvedere, Gorgolesco, and della Torraccia - formed a formidable four-part mountain complex, a critical segment of Field Marshal Albert Kesselring's defensive Gothic Line and a barrier to the U.S. Fifth Army's northward advance during the Italian Campaign.

The fourth and final piece of Kesselring's mountain death trap was the approach to—and eventual assault on—Mount della Torraccia. Mount della Torraccia—linked to Belvedere by a saddle ridge, anchored the eastern flank of the German defensive position.

This map illustrates the coordinated assault designed by Major General George P. Hays, targeting Field Marshal Albert Kesselring's fortified mountain complex.

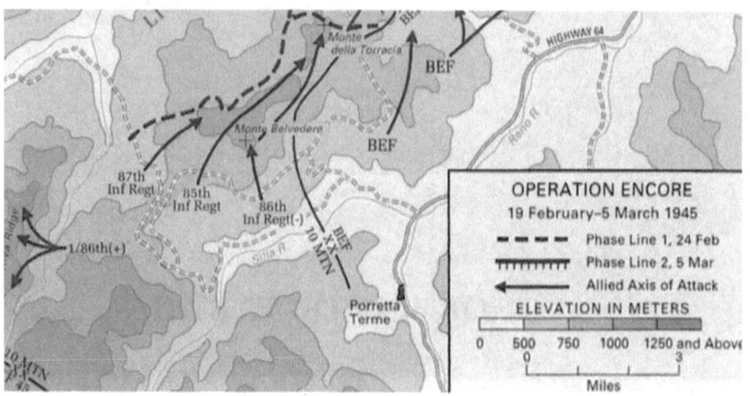

Map: Operation Encore

Though the 2nd Battalion, 85th Mountain Infantry had been held in reserve during the initial night assault on Mount Belvedere (19-20 February 1945), it was quickly thrust into combat on 21 February, once the Belvedere-Gorgolesco summits had been sufficiently secured.

Advancing toward Torraccia under intense, overlapping German artillery fire-from reverse-slope howitzers and ridge-line strongpoints-the battalion faced lethal terrain with little to no cover. German gunners had pre-sighted every likely approach.

It was a second ring of fire.

Pinned down for more than 36 hours, the 2nd Battalion ran critically low on ammunition and water. Under constant bombardment and counterattack, they suffered mass casualties-nearly half their effective strength. Though they hadn't led the initial charge, they bore the brunt of the continued offensive, pushing into some of the deadliest ground of Operation Encore.

With their advance stalled just 400 yards from the summit, General Hays ordered the 3rd Battalion, 86th Mountain Infantry forward.

Late on 21 February, the 86th's 3rd Battalion moved up

under fire, supported by artillery and the 126th Engineer Battalion. Though they didn't immediately seize the peak, their arrival helped stabilize the front and relieve the battered 85th.

On the morning of 24 February, the 86th's 3rd Battalion launched the final assault and, after suffering heavy casualties, captured Mount della Torraccia breaking the last major strongpoint of Field Marshal Kesselring's Alpine defense.

Jim Looby, my late father, served in the 85th Regiment, 3rd Battalion, Company I, known as the I-85th. His battalion led the central assault over treacherous terrain, pushing directly toward the summit of Mount Belvedere.

Alongside the 87th's 1st and 2nd Battalions on the west flank and the 85th's 1st Battalion on the east, the 3rd Battalion of the 85th fought through a punishing ring of fire and captured the German stronghold atop Mount Belvedere.

This story is, in part, my way of honoring him—and the thousands of 10th Mountain Division soldiers who fought beside him. It's also for their families, their descendants, and especially for Jim's grandchildren, who never had the chance to meet him.

He was a wonderful man.

Never in the field of human conflict was so much owed by so many to so few.

Winston Churchill

THE TENTH SERIES

Your Next Trail Mark

Reviews are the trail marks that guide new readers to a story. If Johnnie's journey inspired you, a review on Amazon will help keep the legacy of the 10th Mountain Division alive.

Like a ripple on Mirror Lake, even a single sentence can travel a long way and help honor these mountain soldiers.

Thank you for traveling this trail with me.

→ Leave Your Trail Mark Here:

The Tenth Series

THE TENTH STATION (World War I — Standalone Prequel) 1918, France. Lieutenant George "Price" Hays makes a harrowing ride that earns him the Medal of Honor—but it is his choice between a colonel's daughter and a brilliant librarian that will define the man he becomes.

THE TENTH TRAIL MARK (World War II — The Climb) Twenty-seven years later, that officer—now a general—guides a new generation. Johnnie Grey faces the "unscalable" Riva Ridge, fighting not just for victory, but for the West Virginia farm girl whose silver cross he wears against his heart.

THE TENTH COMMAND (World War II — The Epic Conclusion) The trail ends here. As General Hays orders a desperate night attack to break the Gothic Line, Ranger Colonel Will Darby seeks atonement. Guided by Annie, a British codebreaker who sees the man behind the legend, they must close the gate—to bring their men home.

goodreads.com/joe_looby
amazon.com/dp/B0FXXR4MVW

EPILOGUE

More than a leader, Major General George P. Hays was the trailblazer the 10th Mountain Division needed. His legend was forged in the fire of World War I, where he earned the Medal of Honor for preternatural courage.

Decades later, as a commander of artillery, Hays would again plunge into the crucible of war, landing on the beaches of Normandy on D-Day plus one. The fight to push inland on Day 2 was every bit as savage as the initial landings; Allied troops crashed against deeply entrenched German defenses in a landscape perfectly designed for defense—a maze of dense thick hedgerows, fortified farmhouses, and mined fields.

What follows are General Hays's words, written in a letter shortly after the campaign, reflecting on the men he commanded and the battles they fought.

An Excerpt from the Letter of Major General George P. Hays

HEADQUARTERS

10TH MOUNTAIN DIVISION
APO 345 U.S. ARMY
Italy, 14 May 1945

DEAR MR. DOUGLAS:

Now that I have a few minutes to spare during the whirlwind life we have all been leading since our jump of a month ago, I want to write you more fully of the operations of this Division to date. Have just re-read my short note to you of May twelfth which, on second reading, seems to be curt and ungracious which I assure you was unintentional. I thought you might like me to summarize what I consider to be the highlights of the operations of the Division, as follows:

I personally participated in the Battle of the Marne and the Meuse Argonne offensive in the last war; in the Battle for Cassino with the 34th Infantry Division–landing on Normandy on D plus 1 with the 2nd Infantry Division, the subsequent break through in Normandy, the attack of the fortress of Brest. Also witnessed part of the fight in the Anzio beachhead. As I have told my men, the battles of the 10th Mountain were as strongly contested and as bitter, and in many instances more intense than any I had experienced hitherto.

During our operations we were invariably opposed by the major elements of two or more German first rate divisions. We completely destroyed the five divisions, marked by an asterisk, as effective combat units. The German divisions which opposed us in various phases of our operations were, *232 Infantry Division, *114 Jaeger Division, *2nd Panzer Grenadier Division, *334 Infantry Division, *90 Panzer Division, *94 Infantry Division, 8th Mountain Division, 65th Infantry Division, and 305th Infantry Division. With their supporting troops my one division has been opposed at some time throughout the entire operations by approximately 100,000 German troops.

Lieutenant General Von Senger who commanded the 14th Panzer Corps (emissary whom I delivered to Fifth Army Headquarters in regard to the surrender), congratulated me on having a very fine division, the best he had encountered on all fronts (Russia, France, and Italy). He stated that my division broke completely through two German Panzer Corps and forced himself personally and his staff and many of his troops to swim the Po River on the same day that we crossed in assault boats.

The Commanding General of the 90th Panzer Division, on a statement to his troops, said that in their surrender they had the consolation of surrendering to a very worthy opponent, the 10th Mountain Division.

The Division has encountered and overcome every type of natural obstacle as follows: innumerable rugged mountains of the Apennines and Alps, Po and Adige Rivers, canal region of Po Valley and Lake Garda, also every type of artificial obstacle, to include the old walled city of Verona and pre-war frontier defenses of the Italian-Austrian border along Lake Garda; and one of the toughest positions I oversaw taken was four mutually supporting tunnels with precipitous mountain cliffs on the right and Lake Garda on the left. We took these tunnels by an amphibious movement of a company, in slow moving "Ducks," which captured them from the rear in one of the most daring operations I have ever witnessed.

During our entire operations our Division always had one flank exposed and during the last operation of April fourteenth on had both flanks and frequently our rear exposed. The Chief of Staff, of our IV Corps, stated to me that our crossing of the Po River was one for the record. I was attacking on my right and left flanks, defending my rear and crossing the Po River simultaneously.

As I told my troops, in a recent talk I gave them when the Germans surrendered, no one except those in the Division will ever believe them when they get back home and discuss the operations we have been through. We had a British Lieutenant Colonel Freeth commanding the 178th Lowland Artillery Medium attached to us. He told me that he had supported seventeen British and U.S. Divisions during the war; and that the 10th Mountain was outstanding in its aggressiveness and boldness in taking objectives. He is trying to get permission to identify his regimental insignia with the 10th Mountain Division so as to have lasting recognition for his support of our operations.

As you see from the above, I am very proud of the magnificent work of my gallant soldiers, and am happy that there are people like yourself interested in seeing that they get the recognition due them.

Sincerely yours,

(Signed) GEORGE P. HAYS

Major General, U.S. Army

AFTERWORD: THE RIPPLE EFFECT

Main Street in the Village of Lake Placid overlooks Mirror Lake, a deep, dark pool of clear water that shimmers in the light. In the stillness of early morning, as mist rises from its surface, a single skipped stone can send ripples across the entire expanse, each one reaching for the farther shore.

Some historians might argue that what the 10th Mountain Division achieved in Italy was a small ripple in the vast ocean of World War II. But that ripple, from the courage of mountain soldiers on the sheer cliffs of the Apennines, and the ripples from countless brave Allied soldiers, sailors, and marines across the globe, refused to fade.

It gathered momentum with the force of a snowball rolling down a mountainside, growing larger and more unstoppable with every hard-won peak.

The 10th overcame every conceivable obstacle and its relentless 114-day push spearheaded the Allied advance, helping to trigger the collapse of Germany's southern front and forcing the war's first massive surrender: nearly one million Axis troops in Italy and Austria laid down their arms.

This hard-won victory, however, left an indelible mark. In

just 114 days of combat, the division suffered nearly 5,200 casualties. 992 men made the ultimate sacrifice, their memory forever etched into the very mountains they conquered.

This massive surrender was not merely a crack, but the first torrent released from the dam, unleashing a cascade of capitulations.

Two days after those million Axis troops laid down their arms, another million surrendered to the British in the north.

Four days after that, Germany itself surrendered unconditionally to the Allies.

Sometimes, when the world holds its breath, it takes acts of impossible courage to change its course—like the charge led by the phantoms of the 10th Mountain Division in World War II.

The timeline of the war's end reveals the astonishing speed of this ripple effect:

Historical Notes on the Final Surrenders:

The final weeks of the war in Europe saw a rapid succession of large-scale capitulations, culminating in the complete defeat of the Third Reich. The command structure of the Allied forces was divided by theater, with the Italian Campaign falling under the Allied Force Headquarters (AFHQ), while the campaign in Northwest Europe was directed by the Supreme Headquarters Allied Expeditionary Force (SHAEF).

The Surrender in Italy (2 May 1945):

Having pierced the German Gothic Line, the 10th Mountain Division spearheaded the final Allied offensive in Italy. And their decisive breakthrough in the Apennines catalyzed the final push by the multinational U.S. Fifth Army—which crucially also included the Brazilian Expeditionary Force (BEF)

—and the British Eighth Army. The 10th's relentless advance to Lake Garda helped to sever the last primary Axis escape route, leading to the strategic encirclement of German Army Group C by the Allies.

The strategic encirclement of Axis forces led to the unconditional surrender of the entire German Army Group C, signed at the Allied Force Headquarters in Caserta on April 29, 1945, taking effect on May 2. The immense capitulation totaled nearly one million Axis troops in Italy and parts of Austria. This figure included the 500,000 to 600,000 soldiers in encircled field armies, as well as all rear-echelon and support personnel.

The Surrender at Lüneburg Heath (4 May 1945):

At his headquarters on Lüneburg Heath in northwestern Germany, British Field Marshal Bernard Montgomery accepted the unconditional surrender of all German forces in Holland, northwestern Germany, and Denmark. This capitulation involved an estimated one million soldiers, many of whom were desperate to surrender to the Western Allies to avoid capture by the advancing Soviet Red Army.

The Final German Surrender (7-8 May 1945):

The final, overall "Act of Military Surrender" was signed by German Colonel General Alfred Jodl on behalf of the German High Command at SHAEF headquarters in Reims, France, on May 7, 1945. The surrender was made unconditionally to the Allied Expeditionary Force and simultaneously to the Soviet High Command, with the cessation of all hostilities taking effect at 23:01 Central European Time—5:01 PM in Lake Placid, New York—on May 8, formally ending the war in Europe.

LAKE PLACID NEWS

May 9, 1945

Victory in Europe: Village Bells Ring Out in Joyful Chorus

Yesterday at 5:01 p.m., news of Germany's surrender sent a ripple of pure joy across Lake Placid. The fire siren wailed and church bells, once tolled solemnly for D-Day, now rang out in a triumphant, continuous peal of peace for Victory in Europe, V-E Day.

On Main Street, stunned silence gave way to spontaneous cheers as residents poured from shops and homes. The long-held tension of the war years finally broke in a shared wave of relief as strangers embraced, celebrating late into the evening.

For many, the bells were an answer to prayers, honoring the sacrifices of local sons. Their courage, whether on foreign peaks, on distant seas, or in the air, was proven in the fight, and hastened this victorious day.

Yet, this profound relief was tempered by the solemn knowledge of the war still raging in the Pacific. Even as Lake Placid celebrated, its prayers remain with those still fighting, with the wounded, and in memory of the fallen, awaiting their own day of victory and homecoming.

Last night's celebration was for a promise fulfilled; the village's prayers now turn to the Pacific, awaiting the day of final, total victory.

THE TENTH TRAIL MARK: A DISCUSSION TRAIL GUIDE

This guide is designed to enhance your experience with *The Tenth Trail Mark.* Use these questions and themes to explore the novel's powerful messages of courage, leadership, and the human spirit.

Contents

The Three Crosses

This section invites discussion on the profound symbolism of the three crosses that mark Johnnie's journey: those he encounters and those he wears.

- **The Swiss Cross (National Ski Patrol):** Chosen by the NSP for its neutrality, visibility, and association with safety, this white plus sign on a red background symbolizes guidance and protection.
- **The Crossed Bayonets (10th Mountain Division):** This emblem indicates a light infantry unit trained for close combat and maneuver warfare. The bayonets symbolize the division's combat readiness and fighting spirit. Their crossed form intensifies the idea of unity, strength, and an offensive posture.
- **The St. Andrew's Cross (Saltire):** This "X" shaped cross represents faith and sacrifice. It is also used in rescue and hazard contexts, such as railroad crossings and emergency signs, as a warning sign.

Heroes and Sacrifice

This guide explores the profound nature of heroism and sacrifice in "The Tenth Trail Mark," tracing its themes from the Prologue's account of First Lieutenant George P. Hays to the Epilogue's reflection on Major General George P. Hays and the 10th Mountain Division. As the author notes, "Sometimes, when the world holds its breath, it takes acts of impossible courage to change its course..."

- **The Nature of Courage:** The Prologue and Epilogue feature First Lieutenant George P. Hays and Major General George P. Hays, respectively. What do these bookends tell us about the nature of courage, selflessness, and the sacrifices individuals make for the greater good? How does the story portray the immense and lonely burden of command?

- **Hays's Enduring Spirit:** How does Hays's unwavering determination in the face of overwhelming odds resonate throughout the narrative, particularly in how his experiences define heroism?
- **Leadership in Crisis:** General Hays's assault on Mount Belvedere was a victory achieved at a terrible cost. Discuss the complex morality of his command. Where is the line between strategic necessity, acceptable losses, and heroic sacrifice?
- **Unsung Heroes: Women in the Story:** Beyond the battlefield, how do the women in the story forge their paths of heroism? Despite the societal expectations of their era, how do women like Johnnie's mother, Allee, and Ellie demonstrate resilience and contribution to the fabric of life? Provide specific examples from the book.

1. **Johnnie's Mother:** Her tireless efforts as a seamstress, using a barter system to provide for her family, and her unwavering dedication to homeschooling Johnnie are acts of quiet heroism, ensuring survival and a future despite the Depression's grip.
2. **Allee:** As Johnnie's younger sister, Allee grows into a capable young woman, becoming the new schoolteacher and actively supporting the Red Cross. Her commitment to education and community service showcases her resilience.
3. **Ellie:** Ellie's love for Johnnie and her unwavering faith serve as a heroic force, inspiring him throughout his journey.

a. **Quiet Confidence and Connection to Land:** Her deep connection to the land is evident as she speaks of the "quiet dignity of work."
b. **Support and Sustenance:** Her family's farm provides essential food for their community and the soldiers, a vital contribution to the war effort.
c. **Symbolic Guidance:** Her gift of the St. Andrew's Cross serves as a "trail mark" guiding him home, a constant reminder of what he was fighting for. She wasn't the mission; she was the reason.

- **Heroism Across Time:** Times change, and with them, the face of military service. The 10th Mountain Division today proudly includes thousands of female soldiers who continue to embody courage and commitment. How does this evolution in service reflect a broader understanding of heroism, building upon the rich legacy of the past?

The Trail Marks of a Mountain Soldier

From the quiet forests of the Adirondacks to the war-torn peaks of Italy, Johnnie Grey's journey is not a straight line but a winding path marked by formative moments. The author uses the metaphor of a "trail mark"—a sign that guides a traveler—to frame the key events, lessons, and relationships that shape Johnnie's character.

These ten 'trail marks' are the pivotal moments that forge Johnnie Grey into the man he becomes. For each turning point, discuss how the experience changes Johnnie and prepares him for the challenges ahead.

1. **The Slingshot & The Silver Bullet**

- Summary: Johnnie's childhood is marked by a relentless pursuit of survival through hunting. His handcrafted slingshot and prized "silver bullet" teach him patience, precision, and the value of a single shot. This self-reliance forms the bedrock of his skills.
- Quote: "He had a single steel ball bearing polished to a gleam; he called it his 'silver bullet.'... Each shot counted."
- The Lesson: Self-reliance, intense focus, and the weight of every action.

2. **The Snowball Fight & Meeting Darby**

- Summary: During a chaotic snowball fight, Johnnie employs tactical movements and meets Edgar "Darby" Darby, who mirrors his actions. This event marks Johnnie's shift from a solitary hunter to a team player.
- Quote: "This wasn't just a snowball fight; it was their war, and they were fighting it together."
- The Lesson: The first instance of tactical thinking and teamwork.

3. **Rolf Monsen & The Secret of "Falling"**

- Summary: Mentored by world-class skier Rolf Monsen, Johnnie learns that the secret to greatness is "falling"—that one must push limits, fail, and learn from that failure.
- Quote: "Mr. Monsen... 'what's the secret to becoming a great skier?'... 'Falling!' Rolf shouted back... 'The secret is falling!'"

- The Lesson: A mentor teaches that greatness comes from embracing challenges.

4. **The Lake Placid Ski Patrol**

- Summary: Joining the Ski Patrol formalizes his mountain skills for community service. It is his first official role as a protector, where he applies his survival skills to help others.
- Quote: "When the weather turned foul... It was Johnnie they followed, his unerring instinct serving as their compass."
- The Lesson: The transition from self-preservation to service.

5. **Rescuing the Lost Boy Scout Troop**

- Summary: When a Boy Scout troop is lost in a blizzard, Johnnie finds them and takes command, using his knowledge to keep them alive. It is his first true test of leadership under pressure.
- Quote: "Driven by Johnnie's calm urgency, the boys sprang into action, their fear momentarily eclipsed by a sense of purpose."
- The Lesson: Proving himself a leader in a life-or-death situation.

6. **The CCC & The Wilmington Trail**

- Summary: In the Civilian Conservation Corps, he built the Wilmington Trail. Symbolically, he is no longer just following trails but creating them, painting the blazes that will guide others.

- Quote: "He understood... some marks were more than just paint on a tree; they were promises to others of safe passage."
- The Lesson: Symbolic shift from following trails to building them for others.

7. **Seneca Rocks & The Art of "Holding On"**

- Summary: At the Army's climbing school, he develops a philosophy that complements "falling": the secret to climbing is "holding on." This, with the discipline of silent climbing, forges the trust and stealth critical to his survival.
- Quote: "Here at the rocks, it's not about falling. It's about *holding on*... That's when you learn something real—about the rock, and yourself."
- The Lesson: Physical and emotional endurance is forged.

8. **"The Squirrels"**

- Summary: Devastated by Darby's death, Johnnie is inspired by his friend's final letter warning against the "positive danger" of routine. Facing the "ring of fire" on Mount Belvedere, he develops the "straight run" tactic, based on his memory of hunting squirrels, and defies instinct to save his men.
- Quote: "This is our new instinct... We get out of it. Fast. Straight... Minimize exposure. That's the only way through this."
- The Lesson: Intuition over convention, transforming grief into bold leadership.

9. **The First Shot on Riva Ridge**

- Summary: The final trail mark before his ultimate test is the single, silent shot to eliminate the German sentry. This act is the culmination of his journey: the quiet stealth of Seneca Rocks, the precision of his "silver bullet," and the courage of a soldier.
- Quote: "The shot wasn't the mission. It was a key."
- The Lesson: The culmination of skills that make Johnnie a mountain soldier.

10. **Ellie & The Tenth Trail Mark**

- Summary: Meeting Ellie provides Johnnie with a powerful emotional anchor. She represents a future worth fighting for. Her love and the St. Andrew's Cross she gives him become his final, most important trail mark—the one that guides him home.
- Quote: "You are my tenth trail mark - you brought me home."
- The Lesson: Love and faith become Johnnie's ultimate spiritual compass.

Faith, Hope, and the Spiritual Journey

The novel is woven with spiritual undercurrents. Discuss how faith and hope function as a guiding force in the narrative using the following questions:

1. **The Promise of 'See You at the Top':** How does this phrase evolve from a challenge between friends to a spiritual promise of reunion and hope?
2. **A "Calling":** Johnnie feels a 'calling' to join the war and later to lead his men. Do you interpret this as a call to duty, a spiritual pull, or both?

3. **A Leap of Faith:** In what ways is the 'straight run' through the 'ring of fire' both a literal and spiritual leap of faith?
4. **A "Wink from God":** Ellie believes coincidences are God's way of reminding us to have faith. Where do these 'winks' appear in the story, and how do they guide or reassure Johnnie?
5. **Love as the Ultimate Guide:** How does Johnnie's love for Ellie serve as his ultimate 'trail mark,' providing him with the will to survive and find his way home?

The Ten Mirrors

Main Street in the Village of Lake Placid overlooks Mirror Lake, a deep, dark pool of clear water that shimmers in the light. The novel uses these 'mirrors' to contrast key moments and reveal character growth. For instance, comparing Johnnie's shot with the 'silver bullet' to the first shot on Riva Ridge shows his evolution from a boy surviving to a soldier commanding a battlefield.

Discuss the other mirrored pairs on this list:

1. **The Two Shots:** The Silver Bullet & The Riva Ridge Sentry
2. **The Two Charges:** The Snowball Fight & The "Squirrel Run"
3. **The Two Mentors:** Rolf Monsen & Technical Sergeant McCaffrey
4. **The Two Trails:** The Wilmington Trail & The Recon Ropes on Riva Ridge
5. **The Two Rescues:** The Boy Scout Troop & The Squad on Belvedere
6. **The Two Fathers:** Johnnie's Father & Dr. Darby

7. **The Two Crosses:** The St. Andrew's Cross & The 10th Mountain Patch
8. **The Two Commanders:** Lt. George P. Hays & Johnnie Grey
9. **The Two Worlds:** The Great Depression & World War II
10. **The Two Lakes:** Mirror Lake & Lake Garda

The Ripple Effect

The Afterword introduces one of the novel's most significant themes: the idea that a single, courageous act can create a "ripple effect" with consequences that stretch far beyond the initial event. The novel argues that the 10th's "impossible" victory in piercing the Gothic Line was a decisive blow that accelerated the Allied victory.

As the author notes, "Sometimes, when the world holds its breath, it takes acts of impossible courage to change its course —like the charge led by the phantoms of the 10th Mountain Division in World War II."

- **Reflect and Discuss:** Considering the profound impact of 'trail marks' and 'ripple effects' explored in the novel, how do these concepts apply to heroes in our own lives or recent history who have left a lasting positive impact?

The Spark of Inspiration

An epiphany, or "spark of inspiration," is a sudden and powerful moment of realization. Often triggered by extreme pressure or danger, it's a breakthrough that defies instinct and conventional thinking, leading to a decisive, high-stakes action.

In the chapter "The Squirrels", Johnnie experiences such a

moment—a flash of clarity amid the immense pressure of the "ring of fire." This insight emerges from the convergence of his life's experiences.

As a group, discuss the factors from Johnnie's past that shaped this decision. Identify the **top three most critical factors**, and then decide which one was the most transformative.

1. **The Sand Table and Topographical Expertise:** His experience with the Civilian Conservation Corps allowed him to analyze the terrain model and realize that even General Hays's unconventional plan would stall at the fortified summit, necessitating a more radical approach.
2. **Witnessing the Carnage on Belvedere:** The devastating casualties suffered by the 85th and 87th Regiments proved that existing tactics were failing, creating an urgent need for a completely new strategy.
3. **Darby's Warning:** His best friend's final letter, quoting Clausewitz that "routine... becomes a positive danger" in war, gave him the intellectual framework to challenge his combat instincts.
4. **The Squirrel's Logic:** He reversed the logic (another mirror) he learned as a boy hunting squirrels. He realized their zig-zag survival tactic worked against a single predator but was a death trap in an area of saturation bombing, where minimizing time in the kill zone was the only answer.
5. **Rolf Monsen's Philosophy of "Falling":** His ski mentor's lesson—that greatness comes from pushing limits and finding new ways past them—gave him the courage to abandon "safe" but failing methods.

6. **Seneca Rocks and "Holding On":** His climbing training instilled the unwavering mental and physical grit required to execute a physically grueling, high-stakes maneuver under extreme pressure.
7. **The Chaplain's Sermon:** The chaplain's story of St. Andrew, "forging a new path," provided the moral and spiritual justification for defying conventional wisdom.
8. **The Snowball Fight: An Early Lesson in Unconventional Tactics:** This childhood memory was an early, instinctual lesson in using unconventional, erratic movement to succeed against a larger, converging force.
9. **His Father's Death:** The story of his father's death from mustard gas—an indiscriminate, suffocating threat—created a powerful, personal parallel to the "ring of fire," reinforcing his belief that the only way to survive such a threat was to move through it as quickly as possible.
10. **Ellie's Love as a Guiding Force:** Ellie served as his ultimate emotional and spiritual anchor. The cross and her faith became a tangible symbol of hope and a reason to survive, giving him the internal fortitude to take a profound leap of faith.
11. **From Boyhood Dream to Battlefield Reality:** His childhood fantasy of being an inventive soldier who could save his father was realized in a different way on Belvedere, where his unique life experiences allowed him to save his men.

ACKNOWLEDGEMENT

This journey, much like a challenging mountain ascent, has been profoundly shaped by those who marked the trail before me—teachers, mentors, and trailblazers whose wisdom and encouragement have consistently illuminated the rugged path. Though countless individuals deserve thanks, I wish to specifically honor a few whose guidance has been a particularly luminous beacon. Foremost among them is Nancy Looby, my mother, an unwavering inspiration and a radiant source of light in my life. The legacy of my father, Jim Looby, and his 10th Mountain Division brothers also forged an indelible and guiding mark on my spirit. Their stories and historic adventures vividly shared at reunions—most notably in Vail, CO (1977) and Cranmore, NH—were formative in my upbringing. To my sister, Sarah, and my brother, James, thank you for being the two most remarkable trail marks in my life, consistently illuminating the path ahead and making the ascent easier by walking before me. My wife, Connie, and our children, Kate, Jack, and CJ, have always been a constant source of strength and joy. Our memorable ski trips and hikes, especially along the Wilmington Trail and through the High Peaks, not only revealed the enduring beauty of Lake Placid and Whiteface Mountain, but also the profound bond of shared adventure and love. My gratitude extends to my first-grade teacher, Ms. Ely, who noticed my early struggles with reading and dedicated time after school to help me. I also sincerely appreciate my late Scoutmaster Robert "Bob" Conklin and the entire Stratton

Mountain, VT, Boy Scout Camp family for instilling in me the enduring values of leadership, resilience, and brotherhood. The early camaraderie of the Manning Boulevard crew taught me the simple joys of boyhood fun. The path continued with the sunlit days of lifeguarding, where laughter and teamwork with my companions were a source of pure joy. At Fordham University, the Jesuit professors, through their heartfelt and engaging stories, deepened my understanding of the hardships of the Great Depression, revealing the profound human resilience and societal challenges that test its limits. My service in the U.S. Navy alongside my old comrades instilled in me the understanding that character is defined by service and sacrifice. Professionally, the camaraderie of the DEC gang, the FTI team, and the Sedona Conference pathfinders powerfully affirmed that shared passion conquers any summit. Beyond professional ties, to my dear friends—Jason R. Baron for helping me start the next chapter in life, and the Montclair/914 gangs (because you are amazing)—your collective friendship has been a faithful and steady light. To these remarkable individuals and groups—the "trail marks" on my life's ascent—and to the countless others, often unseen, who illuminated and guided my way forward, I offer my deepest, heartfelt thanks. This journey has also been enriched by inspiration from music, such as New Order's 'Love Vigilantes'—a song that resonates deeply and one I know my old friend Johnnie would have loved. With enduring gratitude for every step shared on this trail.

See you at the top!

ABOUT THE AUTHOR

About The Author

Joe Looby, author of *The Tenth Trail Mark*, draws on a lifetime of mountain adventures and a legacy of military service to craft compelling historical narratives. An avid outdoorsman, U.S. Navy veteran, and Eagle Scout, Joe's work is profoundly inspired by his late father, Jim Looby, a 10th Mountain Division World War II veteran and recipient of the Bronze Star and Purple Heart. Through *The Tenth Trail Mark*, his company 10th Mountain Films, and acclaimed documentaries such as *The Year of the Tiger: JFK 1962* (2016), Joe brings history to life.

He resides near Charleston, SC, with his family but gets to Lake Placid, NY—a vital source of inspiration—as often as he can. A highlight of these journeys, captured below, is standing on the summit of Whiteface Mountain, where you can see the great Lake Placid in the valley below.

One family pilgrimage in 2014 is especially memorable. Intent on "earning" the summit of **Whiteface Mountain,** Joe led his wife Connie and their two oldest kids Kate (11) and Jack (9) up the seven-hour Wilmington Trail.

Cresting the final ridge, the children stared in disbelief at tourists who had driven the Veteran's Memorial Highway and were enjoying cupcakes at the top. Despite the kids surprised exclamations ("Dad, there's a road?"), the hike became a cherished Looby legend—and a reminder that the purest trail marks are the ones you leave together.

For Joe, Whiteface also carries deeper meaning, intertwined with his father's legacy. There is a granite memorial on the Little Whiteface summit, reachable by the Cloudsplitter Gondola, that incorporates a 4-foot chunk of **Mount Belvedere.**

The inset bronze reads: "*In tribute to the men of the 10th Mountain Division, this rock was brought by the government of Italy from Mt. Belvedere, scene of the division's greatest battle in World War II. March 1960.*"

Each visit reconnects him to the men whose footsteps he follows both on the page and the mountain, underscoring that it truly is an epic trip, however you ascend.

For the author's website:
TheTenthSeries.com

www.ingramcontent.com/pod-product-compliance
Lightning Source LLC
Chambersburg PA
CBHW021419110726
47901CB00008B/2219

* 9 7 9 8 9 9 9 1 3 0 1 8 1 *